Jericho lunged forward and kissed him.

Kissed him like he *meant* it. It wasn't hard, or brushing and tentative; it was a warm, familiar kiss, deep with a little bit of tongue and Jericho's hand in his hair. They kept kissing for several long, quiet seconds. Kerry's heart beat like one of those clichéd drums he always heard about. He got a melting shiver up his spine, and he actually wanted to lean closer. To Jericho.

Then Jericho pulled back gently, and they sat there breathing hard and staring at each other for a good thirty seconds. Jericho wiped a gentle thumb down Kerry's cheekbone.

"I think you'll be fine out there," Jericho said. "Just follow my lead like right now, and everything will go perfectly."

He kissed me….

Kerry was stunned, like, he could picture those tiny little cartoon birds swirling around his head kind of stunned. Jericho had kissed him. And it had been kind of amazing.

Welcome to
DREAMSPUN DESIRES

Dear Reader,

Love is the dream. It dazzles us, makes us stronger, and brings us to our knees. Dreamspun Desires tell stories of love featuring your favorite heartwarming heroes, captivating plots, and exotic locations. Stories that make your breath catch and your imagination soar.

In the pages of these wonderful love stories, readers can escape to a world where love conquers all, the tenderness of a first kiss sweeps you away, and your heart pounds at the sight of the one you love.

When you put it all together, you find romance in its truest form.

Love always finds a way.

Elizabeth North

Executive Director
Dreamspinner Press

M.J. O'Shea

Marriage of Inconvenience

Published by

Published by
DREAMSPINNER PRESS

5032 Capital Circle SW, Suite 2, PMB# 279,
Tallahassee, FL 32305-7886 USA
www.dreamspinnerpress.com

This is a work of fiction. Names, characters, places, and incidents either are the product of author imagination or are used fictitiously, and any resemblance to actual persons, living or dead, business establishments, events, or locales is entirely coincidental.

Marriage of Inconvenience
© 2016 M.J. O'Shea.

Cover Art
© 2016 Bree Archer.
http://www.breearcher.com
Cover content is for illustrative purposes only and any person depicted on the cover is a model.

All rights reserved. This book is licensed to the original purchaser only. Duplication or distribution via any means is illegal and a violation of international copyright law, subject to criminal prosecution and upon conviction, fines, and/or imprisonment. Any eBook format cannot be legally loaned or given to others. No part of this book may be reproduced or transmitted in any form or by any means, electronic or mechanical, including photocopying, recording, or by any information storage and retrieval system, without the written permission of the Publisher, except where permitted by law. To request permission and all other inquiries, contact Dreamspinner Press, 5032 Capital Circle SW, Suite 2, PMB# 279, Tallahassee, FL 32305-7886, USA, or www.dreamspinnerpress.com.

ISBN: 978-1-63477-527-4
Digital ISBN: 978-1-63477-528-1
Library of Congress Control Number: 2016908291
Published August 2016
v. 1.0

Printed in the United States of America
∞
This paper meets the requirements of
ANSI/NISO Z39.48-1992 (Permanence of Paper).

M.J. O'SHEA has never met a music festival, paintbrush, or flower crown she can stay away from. She loves rainstorms and a perfect cup of tea, beach days, music, bright colors, and more than anything a cozy evening with a really great book.

She is from the Pacific Northwest. While she lives there still and loves it, M.J. has the heart of a wanderer. So she puts all her dreams of far-off places and extraordinary people in her books.

Except for every once in a while when she does what all travelers have to do on occasion… come home.

E-mail: mjosheaseattle@gmail.com

Website: mjoshea.com

Twitter: @MjOsheaSeattle

Chapter One

THE sun hurt. A lot. Jericho Knox rolled over and stared out the open windows of his bedroom, windows that looked out over the scenic vista of Topanga Canyon—trees, craggy rocks, bright goddamn sunlight. He supposed it was beautiful.

He was too hungover to care.

Jericho's phone buzzed impatiently on his nightstand. He took it and was about to throw it against the wall—they'd send him a new promotional model to be seen with soon anyway—when he remembered.

His meeting.

Fuck damn.

Like he had the mental energy for a meeting. He'd barely poured himself in the door at dawn, and it was all of… what… 10:00 a.m.? Lack of sleep or not, he didn't want to miss this meeting. He *couldn't* miss it. After months of bad screen tests or directors who probably didn't want to put up with his shit and found excuses not to cast him, he finally had a part. At least he almost did. He just had to prove he was the right guy.

Hence the meeting with his publicity team to do just that. Jericho had never been fond of the publicity side of his job—especially when that publicity included him eating crow all over the tabloids over an image that he wasn't even fully responsible for.

He picked up his phone. "Hey, Tom."

"You ready? I'll have a car there in five minutes."

"You know, I do own a car. Three of them, in fact, and a motorcycle. I could always drive myself."

Tom made a noise that kind of sounded like a pained whimper, even though Jericho was nearly sure it was supposed to be a laugh. "I think I'd rather get you there in one of my cars."

Code for "I don't think you'll show up if I leave you to your own devices."

Which was usually, well, true. Completely true. Jericho hated all the paperwork bullshit that went with his job. He hated meetings and contracts and hand shaking. He just wanted to *act*. And if this meeting was what he needed to get onto a solid series so he could finally stop pimping himself all over the place, then he'd fucking do it.

"I'll be there, Tom. We're going to WeHo, right?"

"The car will pick you up in five, Jay. I'll see you there."

Jericho sighed. "Fine." He was too tired to argue anyway.

He hung up the phone and shuffled over to the closest pair of jeans. He had a few clean T-shirts left, but it was time to send his laundry out. Jericho pulled on a shirt and the jeans, tucked his hair under a beanie, since there was no way he'd have time to wash it that day, and grabbed his wallet, phone, and keys.

The drive was unfortunately short, just like drives always were heading to things Jericho wanted to avoid, and by the time they pulled into the parking lot under the building, he was sweating from a combination of heat and leftover whiskey. He climbed out of the car, thanked the driver, because it wasn't his fault he'd been paid to shuttle around an obnoxious actor, and headed to the elevator where an impatient Tom was waiting for him.

"Couldn't you have dressed up a little? We need this to go well." Tom rolled his eyes. He was dressed in one of his typical suits—probably cost more than he could afford, but everyone knew it was all about looks in this town.

Jericho wanted to roll his eyes right back. He was *aware*, Jesus. He knew how much he wanted the part—a rookie detective on a gritty but well-received cop show was exactly what he needed to shake his teen ensemble drama past. He might have been a tabloid darling but he hadn't worked in nearly a year, and his bills were piling up, and his house payments were a bitch. He was just tired of being the person they all wanted him to be. Or getting yelled at about it when he inevitably failed.

"My laundry service is coming today. I didn't have anything else to wear." He shrugged.

"Fine. Let's head up. Let me do most of the talking, okay?" Tom said.

Jericho remembered when he and Tom were kind of friends in a kid-brother, older-brother kind of way. Then Tom got married, and Jericho got tired of playing the jock with a heart of gold on a high-school drama with sliding ratings, and things just kind of went to shit. Maybe if he kept his nose clean and got this job, that would change.

The offices were kind of like he remembered. Jericho had only been in there once before, and he'd been a bit drunk at the time, so there wasn't much to draw on, but the picture by the elevator looked familiar. He saw a blonde girl, Tessie or something. He'd been escorted by her to a few publicity things. She wasn't half-bad. She didn't seem to be headed toward the meeting room, though, so Jericho figured he'd be dealing with George. George Jones wasn't his favorite person. George was stuck in the past and seemed convinced that the only way Jericho could be popular was with the season's newest starlet on his arm. Yeah, he wasn't a fan of George.

Tom turned down the hall that he remembered led to the meeting room. Jericho followed without a word. Easier than acting like he felt—which was ready to be anywhere else.

The meeting began, as it always did, with some obligatory ass kissing, hand shaking, and general small talk to pretend they were a lot closer than they were—all things Jericho, even with his genteel Southern upbringing, did *not* excel at. Eventually, though, they got to business. Finally.

Jericho sat with Tom, George, and some other chick and listened to them spout out options to work on his image—charities, sure why not, some events, some photo ops. And then they said it. Girlfriend. Of course. It always boiled down to that. Jericho scowled.

"Why do you always want me with some chick?"

"Not just some chick, not one of your many one-night-stand types. A girlfriend. Sweet and traditional. Romance."

One-night-stand types. Jericho wanted to scream. "I don't have 'one-night-stand types,' at least not with women. You're sitting here judging me for your own hype."

"We're aware it's just an image."

"And now I have to turn around the image you wanted me to have with another... fake image?" There was a reason Jericho wanted to stay in bed. He didn't have the patience for all this crap.

George had thought the skirt-chaser persona would help sell him, make him attractive to the young twenty-something audience they figured would be his demographic. It was the oldest game in the book. He supposed he was a good enough actor to make it believable. Somehow he'd managed to convince the public he'd slept with every blonde in LA. He knew women found him hot, and he used that and his image to get things that probably weren't good for his career—like maybe a little too much partying and not enough work.

And now it appeared it was biting him in the ass. He'd had to fight tooth and nail to convince one director he was capable of playing a no-nonsense cop, when he actually thought he was meant for the role. Playing a detective had to be a hell of a lot easier than playing a player for eight goddamn years. Especially when getting into bed with a girl was the last thing he wanted to do. Ever.

"I know, Jericho. We just think a steady wholesome girlfriend will work—especially since you're going to be playing a stand-up, genuine kind of guy."

"I thought we discussed the fake girlfriend thing already," Jericho said to Tom. He didn't feel like even looking at George.

"We did," George said. "But things change when opportunities come up. You know that, Jay."

"Don't call me that." Jericho was pissed, and he hated when people got all familiar with him when he wanted to punch them. He stared at George. "Isn't some like… public photo ops where I look all wholesome and nice good enough? Sign some autographs, do a few interviews about how I'm ready to get down to work? Maybe hang out with some kids?"

George returned his stare. Jericho had never liked the bastard, but he had to hand it to him—George didn't back down. "You know what my answer is going to be, and you also know I'm right. You've been around for long enough to get the game, Jericho. We can talk about it for an hour, or we can get down to business."

Screw him. He was right, but that didn't mean Jericho had to like it.

"Fine. Who is it?" Rather rip the bandage off while he could.

"We haven't made any selections yet. Do you want us to come to you with options?"

Jericho shook his head. "No. Just pick whoever. I don't give a damn." It would be over in a few months anyway, right? Didn't really matter who the girl was.

He put his head down on the table and closed his eyes. The meeting couldn't be over soon enough.

NOTHING like a Friday to make all of us lose our damn minds….

Kerry Pickering couldn't wait to go home.

It was only about ten minutes until he could shut down his computer and leave, but those ten minutes felt like they ticked away a second at a time at the speed of evolution. He'd had the longest week ever, and it was time for it to be over. He figured it had hit that time about lunch, and he was hours past anything that could be considered lunchtime. Or dinner.

But he worked for one of the most coveted publicists in Hollywood, and that kind of clout had a price—usually for the people like him. George Jones of Jones & Keller Publicity had left for the day around eleven, unlike Kerry, general grunt employee only a few half steps above intern. Kerry figured George was on the back nine by then, or actually at post-golf cocktails. George always told them the best work got done on the golf course and over cocktails. Kerry wondered why it was that he always managed to be the sucker at his desk at closing time, if that was the case.

Because you're new.

If three years counted as new. It felt like he'd been in the trenches of Hollywood warfare for decades.

"Babe, what are you doing tonight?" Tara—blonde, glamorous, beautiful, but irritatingly sweet and friendly so he couldn't hate her Tara—poked her head around the cubicle wall that sort of looked like an office; at least it had after he'd tacked up pictures of his family, the beach at home, and the friends he never had time to see anymore.

"Couch. Netflix. Why?" After the day he'd had, literally nothing sounded better.

"No reason, just chatting. I have to hit that cocktail party tonight, so I might head out soon if I can escape before Abby decides she needs something else."

"Tara!" Abby screeched from her office.

Abby was George Jones's second-in-command. She had her knickers wedged up her butt just a little bit, but other than that, Abby wasn't too bad. Kerry didn't mind her. He did mind her enormous lists of chores.

They tended to come when he most desperately wanted to go home for the night.

"Guess that plan didn't work out." Tara sighed and tossed a waist-length cascade of wavy blonde hair behind her shoulder. "I seriously hate Fridays. Seems like everything blows up when we'd like to get out of this office for a few days."

"No kidding."

"See you Monday?" Tara asked.

"Yeah." Kerry smiled. For the first time in a long time, he didn't have any Saturday duties. It was kind of a huge relief. He wasn't sure what the hell he was going to do with himself, though.

"What do you have left to do before you go?"

He looked at his list from Abby and the list he'd made himself that morning. Miraculously, every single thing was crossed off.

"I think this is it, unless I get a friendly scream from the right corner office as well."

They listened for a few silent seconds and then giggled. "You're off the hook, darling," Tara said. "I, on the other hand, am not. I should make you come with me tonight."

"*No.*" Kerry thought he'd cry if he had to go to an event after the week he'd had. He wasn't a huge fan of them on his best day. "Please, no."

"Nah, I won't even suggest it. Hell, Abby might decide I'm right if I tell her you should go, and then you'll never talk to me again."

"Basically." Anything other than his couch and a coffee table full of snacks sounded like hell on earth.

When he'd first started the job, the thought of a celeb-studded event—B- and C-list as it most likely would be—seemed… glamorous. Amazing. After a few years in the reality of the publicity game, it just sounded like a lot of work.

"Give Cole a kiss from me, okay?"

Cole would probably keel over and die at just the thought of a real kiss from Tara. They'd only met a handful of times, but his brother's obvious crush was adorable and borderline sad. Tara humored him.

"Cole would probably appreciate the kiss if it wasn't filtered through, you know, his brother's lips?"

Tara giggled in the pure Tara way and flounced off, maxi dress trailing behind her.

"Have a good weekend, Kerry!" she called. Loudly.

Wench. He hoped Abby didn't hear her say that and find more things for him to do before he escaped for the longest break he'd had in weeks.

He waited for a good two minutes for the near-inevitable shout, then shut down his computer when nothing happened, grabbed his messenger bag that was thankfully on the light side for once, and slowly crept to the elevator. When the doors opened and he slid into the cool wood-paneled elevator, he breathed a sigh of relief. Free.

KERRY wondered when his dream had turned into such a chore. Being in public relations was what he'd always wanted to do. It seemed so unreal, working with celebrities, organizing parties and events, clinking glasses with movie stars and pop singers. The reality was… like most realities were. A bit of a disappointment. He spent most of his time behind a computer, rather than at functions and sipping martinis on yachts. Instead he tweeted, uploaded Facebook promo, and sent press releases to tabloids and newspapers. He called other publicity teams and combed social media for public remarks to add into reports for his boss. It was the opposite of glamour. But it was a job, and he was convinced that someday he really would love it. Hopefully. He couldn't have been *that* wrong about everything he'd ever wanted to do.

Still, he was happy to escape from his dream job. The relief he felt slipping into his car was palpable—even more, when he started his car and drove out of the building's garage onto a crowded post-rush-hour street.

Kerry was happy to see the sun. He hadn't seen it since that morning. He'd been too busy to go outside and sit on the benches in the courtyard for lunch. He'd just munched at his leftover burrito and clicked away on his keyboard. Kerry supposed that was what he had to thank for getting him out of work just a touch earlier than the rest of the week. He turned on the radio and rolled down the windows.

He flopped his arm out of the car window and let the breeze rush over it. All of a sudden, everything felt way better. Sure, the city was dirty sometimes and sleazy underneath the slick sheen of fame and fortune, but there was something about the Los Angeles sun, the hills, the beaches, the juice bars, the outdoor malls—Kerry couldn't imagine living anywhere else.

"HEY, guys. I'm home!"

Kerry was ready to be back in his sardine can of an apartment. He shared it with his brother, Cole, and one of Cole's friends named Robbie. It wasn't really a big enough apartment for him and two rather large college seniors, but they made it work and had a lot of fun together in the process.

He didn't do much but flop down on their couch and breathe a sigh of relief. The couch smelled a little bit like Cheetos and beer—none of them were quite sure of the couch's origins other than that it had been free on the side of the road—but it was the most comfortable thing on earth, and Kerry didn't know how any of them would live without it. They typically fought over the highly coveted right corner seat, where he'd already parked himself. It was the best spot in the world. He'd be happy to stay there the entire night.

Kerry promised himself some fun for the weekend—a beach trip, dinner with friends he rarely saw, something. But not until morning. He needed to decompress.

The place seemed like it was empty, so Kerry dragged himself off the couch and wandered into the kitchen for a snack. He knew he should take off his work clothes and put on sweats, but that would mean going to his bedroom, which was a whole twenty steps away.

He found some fruit and a bag of cashews and a bottle of water. Felt pretty damn virtuous about it too. Then he dropped his snack on their old pitted coffee table and went back to change, because it was always better to do it before he grew roots on the couch.

I should really go to the gym....

Shit. It had been weeks.

Kerry wasn't like Cole and his buddies, who seemed to live for lifting and cardio. He was an occasional gym surfer at best, but he needed to stay in shape to fit in with the beautiful people. Tara always looked like she'd stepped off a freaking fashion spread, with her perfect cascade of blonde hair and skin sprayed just the right shade of bronze. Abby and Oscar, who worked directly under George, might not be as flashy, but they were their own brand of pretty—well-kept and expensive-looking. Kerry had to do his best not to stick out like the plain, pale sore thumb he was.

He flipped on the TV, and it was on the entertainment channel Robbie liked to watch when he did his stretching in the morning. There was some red-carpet preshow on, he couldn't tell which right away. It was a bit late for awards season, but he figured the celebs loved to get dressed up and show off their goods. Kerry critiqued each look that came by from a publicist's point of view—too quiet, oh God too loud, maybe a bit low cut, gorgeous, glamorous, frumpy, and holy *shit*… Jericho Knox.

Beautiful, broody Jericho Knox.

Kerry didn't like him very much, at least not his public image, which, if Kerry knew anything about how the world of PR worked, was probably a hell of a lot better than reality. He just seemed kind of… like an asshole. A pretty asshole, but an asshole just the same. He had his silky jaw-length hair tied back in a small ponytail, jaw dusted with the perfect amount of scruff, and a suit—Burberry, if Kerry was right—that fit him so perfectly that his tailor deserved whatever awards they were handing out that night. The guy might smolder at cameras like the James Dean he wished he were, and give journalists less than helpful answers, but, hell, he was beautiful.

Kerry knew Knox's rep, though—difficult, out of control, slept with every chick he could get his hands on, sullen, hard to work with. He hadn't had any personal dealings with the guy, and Knox wasn't on his social media roster, but Kerry knew Jones & Keller represented him.

The front door banged open, and Kerry coughed like he'd been caught doing something he shouldn't do and sat up.

"Hey, Bro," Cole said with a grin.

"What you watching?" Robbie asked.

"Just some red-carpet live stream. Gotta be bitchy and check out what the competition is doing."

"Which ones are your clients?" Robbie asked.

"He is," Kerry said. He pointed to where Jericho Knox was just exiting the screen. "Never met him, though."

"That guy's kind of legendary. Total pussy hound. Sweet."

"*Robbie*," Cole said.

They both loved Robbie to death, but he had Stifler tendencies.

"Yeah. I'm kind of glad he's not my responsibility." Although Kerry would love to have *some* real responsibility, a celeb to do real PR for, a break from running Twitter and doing fucking social media diagnostics. He was tired of being the dork behind the computer. He knew he could do better than that. Kerry pointed out a few other celebs as they walked by. "We've got her. Don't be surprised if you see her on a date with an NFL player in a few days. I think her new single will come out soon, so she needs a publicity boyfriend."

"Is it really like that all the time? So fake?" Cole asked.

"Not always, obviously. But, yeah. It is."

"Fucking stupid," Robbie muttered.

He'd never shown much appreciation for Kerry's work.

"It's not all smoke and mirrors, what we do." Which was kind of bullshit, because it pretty much was. "I mean, we do help them get the word out when they've done something for charity, when they need privacy for family matters." But also when they needed to be seen out with another celeb just a little bigger and brighter than they were to get their name out there. It wasn't just romances. Some of the best Hollywood friendships were born in a boardroom. Nothing the public liked better than a pair of adorable famous friends. Except, of course, an adorable famous couple.

"What are you working on right now?"

Kerry cringed. "I honestly probably shouldn't tell you guys. NDAs and all that."

"You always say that. We're not seriously going to tell anyone."

"It is my job, and I'd rather not lose it."

Robbie grunted. Seeing as he was in school to be a physical therapist, he probably didn't have a grasp of the finer details of publicizing a celebrity. He also probably didn't care much about it. All that stuff seemed really glamorous until the paperwork and the contracts were brought out. Kerry could tell them what he did, to be honest. But it sounded a little pathetic when he described it. He'd rather keep his brother and Robbie in at least a tiny bit of awe over his career.

"Do you have to work tomorrow?" Cole asked.

"Actually, no. I'm free. You guys want to hit the beach?" Even though he loved the beaches, he hadn't spent much time there since college. He supposed it was the realities of being an adult.

"Fuck yes. I need a distraction before my anatomy practical," Robbie said.

Robbie and Cole were heading toward graduation. It was almost surreal that his baby brother was about to be a full adult. Robbie too, who had only been around for two years but seemed like part of the family.

"Bad?" Kerry asked.

"Brutal."

IT was nearly dark by the time Jericho got out of bed for the second time that day. It had been an awful morning, and every time he thought about being stuck on another PR date with another girl he didn't even know, he wanted to give everything up. Actually, he wanted to go out and get drunk. Have one more night of freedom before they hooked him up with some random girl for the next few months, which would mean he'd have to be careful where he was seen out contradicting the public story.

There has to be another way....

Jericho had been willing to do just about anything to convince people he was the right guy for the part, and every job came with its share of bullshit—he knew that just as well as anyone else—but it felt like a prison sentence. One he'd have to live for months at a time.

He decided to go out. Hell, why not? Couldn't do any harm to let off steam for a few hours before turning himself in for months of purgatory.

He got in the shower and washed his hair, scrubbed the stench of the previous night and the stickiness of a nap without air-conditioning, and then put on his freshly laundered best jeans and a tight black T-shirt. If he was going to have one last night, better make sure it was a good one, and the jeans never failed to get him at least some club head if not a hell of a lot more.

THE club was dark and a little on the dive side. Jericho figured he should probably frequent places with strict behavior codes and exclusive clientele, but he didn't want even this part of his life to be tainted by the social-climbing Hollywood types who wrangled invites to even the most exclusive gay clubs for the chance of getting ahead. Like he could really do anything for them anyway. He was barely doing enough for himself.

Jericho wound his way through the crowd and up to the bar. He ordered a set of shots, which he planned to drink all himself, and a mixed drink to chase them away. The bartender poured the shots and the drink, and Jericho tossed him a hundred and a long look—hoped it was enough for the bartender to get the picture that it was in his best interest not to tell the tabloids who he'd seen at his bar that night.

Jericho downed the shots one by one, methodically. It wasn't for entertainment, like the pair of young guys, probably barely twenty-one, who were giggling over what looked like some fancy blue shot. It was just to get numb, to forget he was about to become a faithful boyfriend to some boring blonde. He could do it. He just had to get through the summer, smile, take pics, maybe hold some babies and sign some autographs, and then get himself the hell out of there and to Vancouver where he'd finally be free. And working again.

He chugged down the mixed drink too and pushed the glasses all together for the bartender to pick up. He headed to a booth on the corner of the dance floor and waited for the floor to fill and the drinks to hit. Didn't take long for either. Jericho stripped off his jacket and shimmied his way out onto the dance floor. The room was filled with boys and men, mostly the first. He danced alone for a grand total of maybe ten seconds before one of them shimmied up to him. The guy was slight, pale, dark haired, big eyed, and adorable. Exactly Jericho's type.

"Are you even twenty-one?" Jericho asked with a smile.

"Barely," the boy said. "Three days ago."

"I feel like a grandpa," Jericho murmured.

"You're thirty. Like that's old," the boy said with an eye roll. This one recognized him. Usually that would be enough to make Jericho move along. But the guy was cute, and he was drunk, and Jericho didn't care about anything at the moment. "I'm—"

Jericho held his finger up to the boy's lips. They were soft and plush, and he kind of wanted to kiss them. He usually wasn't into kissing with his hookups, though. Must've been the booze. "Let's just dance."

So they danced, and did a few shots, and danced some more. He didn't want to know the kid's name, but he wasn't interested in finding another partner. Jericho liked the way their bodies fit together, wouldn't mind seeing the kid in his bed either, if he were up for bringing a stranger home. He'd look pretty and pale against the sheets. Even prettier with Jericho inside him. Jericho leaned over and sucked a mark into his neck.

"I always knew, I think," the kid murmured. "I knew I'd meet you someday."

"Yeah?" He waited for the creepies to hit him, but they didn't. The kid seemed sweet, not stalkerish.

"Maybe it was just a hope," he said breathlessly. "Can I kiss you?"

"Sure." Jericho was in the mood to break his rules.

They kissed for a while. Jericho didn't really notice time passing. His head was hazy and tired and sloshed with too much tequila. He had no idea how close it was to closing time, but the club was still packed. He liked blending into the crowd, instead of sticking out like he usually did. Sure, he'd gotten some stares, but there was this unspoken rule, somehow. Leave him alone. Jericho liked it. He wrapped his arms around his dance partner's waist and turned him so his back was up against Jericho's chest. They swayed to the music. Jericho ground against the boy and groaned. He tightened his hands, bit his lip, squeezed slight hips.

"C'mon," the kid said.

He felt himself being led down a dark hallway toward the restrooms. It was claustrophobic back there, and Jericho wasn't sure what he thought about it.

"Come in here."

Jericho followed him into the bathroom and an open stall. He let the kid unbuckle his jeans, push them down over his hips, and kneel in front of him. He slapped his hand against the side of the stall when his cock slid into wet warmth. He didn't care about his impending girlfriend, his agent, the publicity team, any of it. He had a hot mouth around his cock, and he was going to come in near seconds if he didn't get a grip. Instead of backing off when Jericho pulled his hair, the kid kept going, harder, faster until Jericho teetered at the edge. It was just as he was going over, shouting out his orgasm, that he heard the faint click of a cell phone's camera shutter.

"Fuck," Jericho groaned. "No, no, no."

His partner pulled off with a satisfied look. "What? Are you okay?"

"Didn't you hear that? Sounded like a camera."

The other guy shrugged. "No. I didn't hear a thing."

Jericho wondered if he was being paranoid. Still. The moment was ruined and he was more than a little spooked.

"I gotta get out of here," he said.

"Okay." He got another shrug. "It was nice to meet you."

"Um…." Did he know the kid's name? No. No he didn't. "You too. Nice to meet you."

Jericho did up his jeans and sprinted out the back door of the club before he threw up all over the parking lot. A quick glance told him nobody was out there to witness it. Safe. Close call, but safe.

Chapter Two

IN the two years he'd been working at Jones & Keller Publicity, he'd been called into George Jones's office exactly once before. And that was to sign his contract. When Kerry got an e-mail to meet his boss after lunch in the office, he was… only mildly terrified. Or a bit more.

Happy Hump Day.

The beginning of the week had been so unusually calm too. They always paid for those days.

He went out for lunch like he usually did with Tara and a distracted Abby, but he couldn't eat. He was too nervous to eat.

"What's the matter, babe?" Tara finally asked. She'd nicked a few of his truffle fries already, even though Kerry knew she'd be moaning and groaning about calories and fat in an hour or so.

"I'm just kind of freaking the hell out internally."

"About what?" Abby looked up from her phone and put her kale-adorned fork back in her bowl of salad.

"I got called into Jones's office for a meeting after lunch. I've never been called into Jones's office. He's totally going to fire me."

Tara giggled. "Why would he fire you? You're adorable, and you're doing a really good job." She tugged on her high, thick ponytail to tighten it and snagged another one of his fries. "Besides, I got the same e-mail, so unless he's firing both of us, you're safe."

"I got the e-mail too," Abby said. She was already looking back at her phone, doing whatever it was Abby was constantly doing.

Kerry had been looking forward to a fun afternoon of promo-tweet composition and maybe a Facebook post or two. All of a sudden, with the others going into the meeting, things didn't seem all that bad.

"Do either of you have a clue what it's about?"

Abby shrugged but didn't say anything.

"I haven't heard anything. I wish he'd just tell us in the e-mails instead of sending out these vague and… what's that word, when it seems like something's going to happen?" Tara asked.

"Ominous?" Kerry said.

"Yeah. Ominous. I wish he'd stop with that shit."

"So he's done this before?" he asked.

"All the time," Abby muttered. "Maybe that means you're moving up in the ranks."

Kerry would kiss George Jones's shoes if it meant he'd actually get to do some publicity work finally, instead of getting coffee and firing off the odd tweet all day. He had an actual university degree. He was better than Twitter.

"That would be amazing. And way better than getting fired."

"I'd imagine most things would be better than getting fired," Abby said. Her voice was its usual tone of disinterested and unimpressed. Sometimes Kerry wondered why she went to lunch with them at all for how much fun she seemed to be having.

"Yes. Most things are."

THEY finished lunch; Kerry actually took a few bites of his chicken wrap and downed his drink—he always got thirsty when he was nervous. Then they walked the three blocks back to the office building where he spent most of his life. Unfortunately.

All three of them shuffled into George Jones's office and sat in the chairs he had clustered around the table he liked to use for meetings. George Jones was a squat man, and unassuming to look at, which came as a surprise to most people since he had about as much power in Hollywood as a king. Everyone wanted his representation. Hardly anyone got it.

"Ladies and gents," he said. He gestured at Abby, Tara, Kerry, and Oscar, who'd just sat down at the table with them. "We have a problem."

All four of them waited silently for Jones to continue. Kerry, for one, planned to say nothing until he was asked to speak. Better that way. Definitely.

"One of our clients needs an image overhaul. He's been signed as a second-season lead on *Steel Street*, but they're threatening to recast if he doesn't clean up his publicity."

"Who?" Kerry asked. Then he remembered he wasn't supposed to speak unless he was spoken to. Jones didn't seem to mind, though.

"Jericho Knox. He needs some good buzz, and he needs it fast."

"You want us to get him involved in some charities?" Abby asked. "Maybe throw a gala or two?"

"People don't care about charities," Jones said. "He needs a summer romance. Something wholesome. Traditional. A whirlwind kind of thing that the public can buy into. He's already signed on to the idea, reluctantly, but it's our job to put it together. Including the perfect girl. So it's go time. Key word 'sweet.'"

Jericho Knox? Sweet?

The last thing Kerry could ever imagine was him being... sweet. Jericho was known for partying, for his womanizing ways, for fast cars, and for his ridiculous cliffside mansion. There was nothing sweet or traditional about him. How the hell were they going to sell that?

"You thinking the usual? Family meet-ups, shopping and coffee, a premiere or two?" Tara said.

"Yes. But don't just check the boxes. I want this to look genuine. I swear people these days are getting better at picking out the couples who are just acting."

Tara nodded. "Check. Make it more unique and believable."

"Yes. And Abby, I want you to clean up his social media—pictures, dickhead tweets, anything that's lingering in screenshots anywhere. You're on duty." Abby nodded. Kerry was surprised that task hadn't been handed to him. "I also want you to get with the media. Set up some headlines, get them ready to play ball."

And then Jones looked at Kerry. "I'm going to have you get me a list. Models, but nothing scandalous, maybe a nice actress who needs some promo, nobody too famous, make sure they don't have any skeletons. He needs a good girl. Nothing flashy." Kerry nodded. "*No* reality-show people. I want someone who will look credible."

"Got it." Kerry's hand shook, and he sat on it to keep it from trembling outright.

"Good. Get with their people. I want a full list of willing potentials. Check our client roster first, obviously."

"Of course."

"What do you want me to do, sir?" Oscar hadn't spoken until then. Kerry wasn't a fan of Oscar. He didn't think anybody was.

"While Pickering is working on that, I need you to take over some of the social media accounts he's been running. He's not going to have a lot of time for a few days."

Kerry almost chuckled at that. Oscar was *not* going to be happy about it.

TWENTY-FOUR hours later, reckoning day had come, and Kerry was anything but ready. He'd gotten his list, talked to publicists, had quite a few more bites than even he had anticipated. Jericho Knox had a huge slew of… well B- and C-list celebs at his disposal—pretty girls who played vampires and witches on primetime TV, a few pop stars, even a fairly well-known athlete who was fishing for a few more endorsement deals to add to her portfolio; they had all said yes. Kerry had headshots, bios, and he'd vetted the families for people who might act like nutcases on the Internet. It was all good to go.

Kerry had never been so nervous.

George would be in the meeting, along with the rest of the team, Jericho's agent, and… Jericho. Even with his job, it would be Kerry's first up-close-and-personal encounter with a celebrity. And what a celeb to start with.

Jericho Knox.

He was the quintessential Hollywood bad boy. He would be a cliché if he didn't pull it off so damn well. He was gorgeous, dark haired, had the most glamorous smile Kerry had ever seen, and was rumored to be a huge spoiled jerk. He'd gone through a ton of agents, according to the rumors, and if he wasn't so good for Jones's portfolio of clients, he most likely would've been dropped from them as well.

His fans loved him, the public seemed to devour his escapades in the latest gossip rags. The industry? They'd had their fill. Still, he'd finally gotten hired and a key role on a new detective thriller was the exact role his brooding brand of good looks was meant for. But they wanted sexy and dangerous, not bratty and hard to deal with. And that's where the publicity came in—with the pretty girlfriend and the whole new package.

Kerry's hands shook as he lifted his neat little package of pretty girls ripe for a few publicity dates and headed down to the meeting room.

His hand nearly slipped off of the styled glass handle of the door, and he almost tripped over the nearly nonexistent kick plate under the door, but Kerry managed to make it into the room without any serious disasters. Thankfully. He cleared his throat quietly and took a seat next to Tara, who was probably the only person in the room capable of making him less terrified instead of more.

You wanted this. You wanted more responsibility. Now you have it.

Now he had it.

It took a few seconds, but Kerry finally forced himself to look up—he knew most of the people, of course, and the other one? Holy hell. There was no mistaking him. Kerry always wondered how much of a celebrity's appeal was makeup and lighting and the best stylists. Maybe for some of them it was, but Jericho, shit, there was just something magnetic about him. He lounged insolently in one of the conference room chairs, in a plain white T-shirt, jeans, leather bracelet, and a pair of Wayfarers holding his dark jaw-length hair back from his face. Kerry wanted to stare. Maybe it was his eyes. Everyone always talked about how big they were, how long-lashed and warm brown and just the kind of eyes that would draw someone in, but Kerry hadn't really bought it—until he was staring right at them, ready to pass out. Tara knocked knees with him under the table, and Kerry looked down immediately.

"Super cool," she whispered.

He started giggling uncontrollably, and it took a coughing fit and a sip of Tara's water for him to chill out. Luckily, that was about the time George walked in, so he missed Kerry's dork fit. But Jericho didn't. He was peering at them disinterestedly, eyebrows raised.

Fuck shit.

Exactly how Kerry wanted to start the meeting.

"So. We have some work to do," George started as he sat. "Jericho. Tom." He nodded at both Jericho and his agent. Kerry realized he hadn't even noticed the agent sitting there in an expensive suit and shiny leather shoes. How the hell was he supposed to notice that guy when Jericho was right next to him.

"Tara, you want to start us off? She's going to run social. Set up events, parties for you to be seen at. We're going for playboy since that's not too much of a departure, but more playboy on the Riviera, less Playboy mansion."

"Yes, and there are some great events coming up this summer. We have Ellen's barbecue on Memorial Day. We've wrangled you an invite with a plus one. That event is always highly photographed. Everybody loves Ellen. We can splash those pictures all over the place. Have you in a nice linen suit, fedora, date on your arm. And there's—"

"Sweetheart, you know all that foofy stuff isn't my scene," Jericho said.

He talked. His voice was surprisingly Southern, a little raspy and low, like melting ice cream and caramel sauce, and, hell, Kerry was being an idiot. But the guy was *sexy*. *He's an asshole. Try not to forget that.*

"It has to be your scene, Jay." His agent nudged him. "Do you want this part or not?"

"Yeah. Okay. Fine." He nodded at Tara to keep going. "I hate it, though. A lot."

"We have a White Party on the Fourth of July, a few premieres in June, a charity ball, some tennis matches—we could fill your calendar from now until it was time for you to leave. Of course, we'd want to leave in some room for casual dates, dinner, coffee, shopping, maybe a Hawaiian vacation, photographed of course. The usual."

"Yes. So natural and not even remotely contrived."

Tara winked at him. "I suppose it's good for all of us that you're an actor."

"I have no idea why the public buys this shit."

"They probably don't. But it still will keep your name out there in a good way. And even if they do? It's just another acting role. Think of it as that."

Jericho sighed.

"And Kerry," George gestured to him, and he thought he might have a panic attack. "Kerry has a list of potentials here."

"George, I don't want to do this PR stunt stuff anymore. I don't need to get married and settle down anytime soon, but I want to live my own life and not be some attention seeker's fake boyfriend."

"I think you're forgetting that those attention seekers are doing you a huge favor right now. You aren't in the position to be annoyed with what we have planned for you. You need this, Jericho."

"I really can't just do some charity and call it a day?"

"I know you know the answer to this. We had this conversation the other day. Do we need to have it again?"

"No." Jericho sighed. He looked honestly angry. Kerry didn't get it. Most of the people, at least from what he'd seen, didn't seem to mind the promo part of the game. They all kind of knew it was just the way things were. He didn't get why Jericho hated it so much.

George gave Jericho a condescending look. "How much does the public usually care about charity?"

"Not very much. They want a story." Jericho's voice reminded him of a student parroting some fact that a teacher had told him a million times.

"Exactly. They want a romance. And we're going to give it to them. Then it can slowly fade while you're away filming, she can say it was wonderful while it lasted but you two grew apart with the distance, and we're golden."

Kerry hated when George said shit like "golden," like he was trying to fit in with his younger clients. George operated best with the high rollers on the golf course. He had probably spent his whole weekend there. Kerry felt bad for his wife.

"You really think the only way I can fix my rep is to date a 'nice girl'?" Jericho even did the little finger quotes.

"I think it's the best and the quickest way, yes. Charity work doesn't get tabloid mentions. Hand shaking at events doesn't either. You already know what people want to read about, what will get your name in their heads in a positive way."

"Yeah. I know."

JERICHO had the same thought he'd had about a million times since the meeting yesterday. Was it worth it? Was any of it worth it? Sometimes he wondered what life would be like if he'd never left home, if he were a lawyer with his dad back in Charleston, stayed out of the spotlight, found a decent guy. Would that have been easier than doing what he loved but putting up with a ton of bullshit?

Probably.

But Jericho was an actor, and as much as he hated the rest of the shit that came along with it, he felt *right* when he was in front of the camera. It felt like a million years since he'd worked, and he supposed dating a girl for the tabloids was just another form of acting. It wasn't like he was going to be the rainbow cop on the show— he'd play straight there too. Wasn't that big of a deal to play straight in real life. Was it? Jericho wondered how long it would take to convince himself. He sure as hell didn't feel okay. He felt like shit every time he saw his name in the tabloids linked to yet another girl. Every time he went home to visit his mom and she wondered when he'd settle down with a nice guy and give her a grandbaby or ten. He just... felt like shit. But he had to do it. At least it was short-term, and soon enough he'd be off in the misty Pacific Northwest and hopefully free of stunts. Hopefully.

"Get a few years of the show under your belt, go for a leading man role, then maybe you and I can talk about coming out." George had always said. *"You know what reality looks like. You know it's getting easier for gay actors to get cast as leading men once they're out of the closet. You also know it's not great yet out there. Especially when you're still working on getting established."*

They'd had the same argument a million times. George wanted him to establish himself as more than a moody supporting actor. Jericho thought he was probably right. Still sucked like hell. So he kept his mouth shut, and he let George set him up with one more fake girlfriend. This time it would be more serious, more cute-couple shit, and he was determined to make sure this one knew he was gay. Right away. The last time he'd done a few PR dates, the girl hadn't known about him, and she'd started thinking they were going to turn into something real, and then he had to tell them the truth about why it couldn't, and then there was all the awkward paperwork binding them from leaking his sexuality to the public in any way and blah, blah, blah. It was a huge pain. Jericho never wanted that to happen again.

"So what now?"

"Now we set it up, take a break over the weekend, and then put the plan into place."

Jericho sighed. "Fine. Plan away."

He glanced over at the younger guy who'd been pretty quiet since he was introduced at the start of the meeting. He was exactly Jericho's type. He really did like the little dark-haired ones. Kerry was a lot prettier than the guy at the club—Jericho shuddered at the memory of his near disaster. His skin was milk pale but dusted at the cheek with a soft rosy flush, and his hair was so black it shone nearly blue in the sun from the window. He was small and compact, but not skinny. Looked like he was hiding a nice ass under those khakis, and he had some muscle on his shoulders.

Gay? Jericho wondered if he'd be the type to indulge in a little bit of extracurricular fun. Probably not; looked a bit like a newbie corporate stiff, but he sure as hell was delectable.

"Can we be done for the day?" Jericho asked. "I have some errands to run." He didn't really, but he'd rather be anywhere than sitting in George's office unless he was making out with the pretty underling, Kerry. And that wasn't likely to happen.

Chapter Three

KERRY woke to the insistent buzzing of his phone. It seemed like every time the damn thing stopped, it would start back up again. He looked at his clock. What the hell? It wasn't even six in the morning yet. Kerry picked up his phone to turn even the buzzer off when he saw a whole slew of texts from Tara. They exchanged jokes and cat gifs occasionally, but nothing like the… *twenty* texts he'd gotten from her in the past fifteen or so minutes. The final one read:

If you're still asleep wake up. Get here. Now. Code really fucking red.

It had just been sent moments before. Kerry hopped up and hit reply.

Getting dressed. Will be there ASAP.

He shoved on the jeans he'd been wearing the night before at dinner with the boys, grabbed a new button-down and a light jacket, brushed his hair, stuck on a pair of shoes—who the hell knew what they were in the dark—and ran out the door. He had to come back for his workbag, but then he ran out again. He knew he looked like a mess. He'd never worn jeans to the office before, and while his feet were telling him that he probably had two of the same type of shoe on, well, he wasn't certain of that either.

THE office was silent when he got there, except for a light in the main conference room and three very tense people—George, Tara, and Abby. The Jericho team. His team.

Tara snorted a little when she got a good look at him. "Nice shoes," she murmured.

Kerry looked down. He had on one navy converse and one green. Fantastic. He was there, and it wasn't even light out yet. The shoes could be dealt with later.

"What the hell is this about?" he muttered.

Abby and George were in the corner with a file and two very serious looks.

"Our boy Jericho kind of fucked it hard core."

Kerry had to admit he was curious, but he was also thirsty. "George, can I go grab a water before we start?" he asked.

Kerry had just gotten used to addressing George directly. He thought he sounded pretty damn chill about it.

"Yes. Of course. Can you get four? I think we're going to have a lot of talking to do."

Kerry went to the refrigerator and grabbed four bottles of water. He also took one of the doughnuts he usually steered far clear of and a piece of fruit. He'd never been more grateful for the stocked pantry that George kept. Looked like it was going to be lunch out that day. If they even had time.

George passed around folders to them as soon as Kerry sat in his spot. Kerry opened the folder and gasped. Not the way he'd thought he'd start his morning, but all of a sudden, the five thirty wake-up call was quite clear.

The picture was of Jericho, of course. The rest of it… came as a hell of a shock. Jericho's face was clear as day in the shot, in the throes of ecstasy, shirt unbuttoned, smooth chest right there skimming down, down, down to where a guy…. A *guy* was quite clearly sucking him off. A man and Jericho Knox. They had to be in a public place. It looked like a restroom or a club or something. But it was a guy—nameless, faceless, and thankfully anonymous, but a guy nonetheless. Kerry was shocked.

"What the hell?" His voice sounded squeaky even to himself.

"I don't know if he did this on purpose—he's been arguing with me about this for nearly a year, but if the child wanted to come out, this wasn't the goddamn way to do it." George let out a frustrated sigh.

"C-come out?" Kerry thought he might have entered an alternate universe sometime between when he fell asleep and when he was woken up by about a zillion texts.

Tara gave Kerry a long look. "Babe. You didn't know?"

"Didn't know what?"

"Jericho is gay."

Abby, George, and Tara all gave him long looks.

"Gay?"

"Completely," Tara confirmed. "But also completely in the closet, at least to the public. He was happy with that arrangement at first, but has grown increasingly less so recently. We'd been working on a plan for him to eventually come out, but—"

"Looks like he did that for you." *Holy shit.*

Fucked-up wasn't even an accurate word for how much trouble Jericho Knox had landed himself in.

"What was all the womanizer stuff?" Kerry was spinning. He knew the answer; it was Closeting 101, and Kerry was a lot smarter than that, but he didn't know what to say and that seemed like something. Sure he'd only had one meeting and years of watching the guy on screen, but he'd never once even thought it, never once had a moment where he thought "what if?"

What if Jericho Knox, greatest playboy ever to hit the small screen and every magazine in the supermarket, was… gay?

If he hadn't been sitting, Kerry would've had to take a seat, or his legs would have given out.

"What are we going to do?"

"We can't deny," Tara said. "There's literally no way this isn't him."

"Pay off the person who took it? Make sure it doesn't get out?" Kerry said weakly.

"Well," Tara cringed. "They didn't come to his team with the picture. They tweeted it with hashtag

Jericho Knox, hashtag time to leave Narnia. It was brutal. And it's all over the goddamn Internet."

That sounded more than brutal. It was *immoral*. "Who would do that?"

Abby looked even more irritated than usual. "We have no idea. Some guy who thought Jericho owed him one after a one-night stand. Someone who wanted the attention. Who knows? Although money's out because they gave the picture away for free. They could've made a hell of a lot of cash off the picture, but it seems like they wanted the information out more than they wanted compensation."

George made a hissing sound. "It doesn't matter, people. The picture is out, no matter how it got there, and we need to get our client in here. This is a goddamn disaster. But before we talk to him, we need a plan."

How on earth are we going to spin this? Kerry wracked his brain.

"What about privacy?" he finally said.

"Privacy?"

"Yeah. I mean…." *Shit, what did I mean?* Kerry tried to think on the spot. "What if… what if this wasn't some club hookup? There's no way to deny Jericho's into men now, so that ship has sailed. But what if we turn this around to make it look like that guy is someone special, that he and Jericho just got caught up in a private moment. Take some of the sleaze off of it, maybe?"

"Do we even know who he is?" Abby asked.

"Does Jericho?" Tara added.

"I don't know, but you can't see the other man's face at all. That might be… a benefit."

"What do you mean, Kerry?" George asked.

"I mean if that guy is nobody, then he could be anybody. Including Jericho's long-term boyfriend. Fiancé even. Let's say they were out for the evening and had a few drinks and got carried away. They didn't know someone was looking. Jericho's privacy was horribly violated, he's the victim here. Yes, he's gay, and he's proud, but now the whole world has seen a private moment between him and the guy he's in love with. We can turn this around."

George pursed his lips. "Not a bad idea."

"We…." Abby looked at the picture. "We'll just need a guy."

"Kerry, I need you to call Jericho in. His number is in my address book, password nineiron62. Tell him to bring Tom. We're going to need a war room."

"We're going to need a hell of a lot more than that," Tara grumbled. "We're going to need a miracle."

JERICHO woke, again, to the incessant buzzing of his phone. It wasn't his alarm, though. He didn't have any plans for that day, other than to get ready for his new girlfriend—whoever pretty, twinky Kerry picked out for him. But his phone seemed to think he did have other plans. He looked. It was Tom.

"What is it, Tom?"

"You're in deep-ass shit is what it is."

Jericho waited. And waited. "Are you going to tell me what it is, or am I going to have to beg to find out what I did wrong this time."

"Get your laptop out and check Twitter. You should find out pretty damn quickly."

Twitter. The bane of Jericho's existence. It was lucky he had his password saved on his computer, or else he'd never be able to even sign on, since he'd long ago forgotten it.

He dragged his laptop over from where it rested on his bedside table and opened the cursed app. That's when he saw his name trending high on the list. Oh, God. What? He clicked on the link and found them – copy after copy of the same thing spattered all over the Internet. A picture of him from the other night, head thrown back, and the little black-haired club kid clearly sucking his dick.

"Oh, fuck," he murmured.

"Yes. Exactly. Fuck. And there's more."

"Lemme guess. *Steel Street* is dropping me?"

"That's the distinct impression they gave me. They said we have a week to clean this up, or else they're going to recast your role. They would've done it already, but they love your chemistry with Wiley."

"So what now?"

"We have a very long, emergency meeting coming your way."

"Tom...." Jericho had already had enough meetings in the past week to last a lifetime. He grunted.

"Jericho, don't blame me for this shit. We're going to dig you out of it, and you'll be on a flight to Vancouver in September, but it's going to be hard, and you're going to have to put your attitude away."

"There's no way I can pretend this didn't happen. I can't go back in the closet after this." He wouldn't. If he had to have his dick out all over Twitter, one damn good thing would have to come of it.

"I don't think that's what they've planned. Not at all."

"So no more publicity relationship?" Jericho said. He was confused. That was George's fix to everything.

Obviously the girl wasn't going to work, but maybe it would. Jericho didn't get how their game worked half the time. "I really didn't want to do that."

"I think you've managed to make it so you won't have to. Get dressed. Get a shower. Look presentable. This isn't a day for attitude." Tom sounded almost angry.

"I didn't think anyone would take a picture of me, Tom."

That's when Tom exploded. "What the hell were you thinking, Jericho? You've been handed a cherry job, perfect for you or for anyone in your position, and you blew it by… getting blown, of all things. Do you even know that guy?"

"No. I didn't even know his name."

"Jesus. I hope it was worth it. We have a week to prove they don't need to recast, but I doubt it'll end there. You're going to have to work your ass off this summer so the director doesn't think you're a liability. We need the public to love you."

"I assume we're going to George's."

"Unfortunately. I don't want to go there today any more than you do. My kid has a soccer game that I'm missing. Thanks for that." Tom was rarely so sarcastic and angry with him.

"Jesus. I really am sorry. I can't even believe…."

Tom sighed. "Just get dressed. I'll pick you up myself in twenty minutes."

Jericho was about to say good-bye when he realized the air was dead, and Tom had already hung up. Damn it.

He moved woodenly from his bed to the shower. He was still in shock—that much was obvious—and disgusted with himself, whoever took that picture, and the dark-haired kid, if he was in on it. The whole situation was a fucked-up mess, and he had no idea how George Jones and his team of trusty spin doctors were going to get him out of it. He didn't think there *was* a way out of it. He hoped they proved him wrong.

CALL Jericho Knox… seriously. Just, call him. Right. Shit, shit, shit.

George should've had him call the agent. Nobody calls the talent. Right. Nobody does that. What the hell? Right? *Right?*

Kerry knew he was spinning. He also knew he had Jericho's phone number right in his hand, and he couldn't think of anything scarier at that moment than calling him. Jericho had to know the scandal had broken. He had to know he was in the middle of the deepest hole of shit he'd been in since his career started. He wasn't going to be in a good mood, it wasn't going to be pleasant, and Kerry had to call him. Maybe he should have had Tara do it. Everyone liked Tara.

Jericho Knox is gay?

It hit him every minute or so, the bald shock when he realized that, yes, he'd completely and totally missed something that big. He wouldn't say obvious, because it wasn't. Not to him. Maybe he'd been too busy noticing how fucking hot Jericho was, so he didn't notice the gay. Because he really didn't. He thought back to the first meeting when Jericho had been slouched in the office chair, all calm and nonchalant but still defensive as hell—Kerry supposed it would've been hard to tell anything about a person in that position.

He's gay. Jesus. Dial the damn number.

He punched out the number to Jericho's cell and crossed his fingers that Jericho wouldn't pick up. It was awfully early. Maybe he was still asleep and hadn't heard he was about to be thrown into the flames of hell. Maybe—

"Hello?"

No maybe there.

"Um, hi. Jericho?"

"Yes? Who is this?"

He didn't sound too overwhelmingly hostile. Things were looking up.

"Hi. I'm Kerry, from Jones & Keller. Mr. Jones would like to set up a meeting today." He'd called it a war room. Jericho probably wouldn't react well to that name.

"I know. My agent is already on the way." He actually seemed a bit tired. Run-down. Kerry figured if he were in that position, tired would be an understatement. "How bad is it?"

"It's not amazing. I think we can fix it." Kerry had to sound positive. Jericho couldn't come into the meeting already sure they couldn't help him.

"I'm not going back in the closet," Jericho grumbled. "This is shit, but I'm out, and I'm staying out."

"Hey. Hey." Kerry's hands shook. He was so not in any position to be the one placating the talent. But here he was. "Nobody said anything about that. They weren't going to. I promise."

"You sure?"

"Yes. I… I won't let that happen, okay? I get it." Great. The grunt worker just made a promise he so can't keep. Except there wasn't anything in the plan about Jericho going back in the closet, and he already knew that.

Jericho chuckled. It sounded a little sour. "You're the cute one, aren't you? With the dark hair and the nice ass?"

"Um. I guess?" Oscar's hair couldn't be called dark, more sandy ginger. Kerry didn't think he was all that cute, though. And it was surreal as hell to have someone like Jericho tell him he had a nice ass. A bit unprofessional, but surreal.

"So you'll protect my honor, then, Kerry?"

"Um, sure. Listen, Mr. Jones would like to have you here by ten. Can you do that?"

"Yes. I'll be there."

"I can call your agent if you'd like."

"No, it's fine. Like I said, he's on his way. We've already spoken today, anyway. At length."

"Okay."

"I'll see you at ten. Kerry, is it?"

"Yes. Kerry."

KERRY hung up the phone and just about passed out. He noticed Tara watching him from her own desk. "On a scale of one to ten, how terrified did I sound?"

"Only about a solid eight." She gave him a sympathetic smile. "You did good, sweetie. Jericho's actually nowhere near as bad as you'd think he is. A bit of a dick and a little self-absorbed, but what celebrity isn't? I've been to a few events with him. He's okay."

"Yeah…."

"Do you need some sugar or something? You look a little pale."

"Breakfast would be nice. And coffee."

The crisis had barely hit, but somehow it seemed like they'd made it through the worst of the storm. He knew there was far worse to come, but his stomach had settled, and they didn't have that much time before the meeting.

"You want to hit Starbucks? I'd love a latte, and we could both use some fresh air."

"Yeah. Starbucks."

Kerry stood and only felt a tiny bit of a dip before everything straightened out in his vision.

"Hey, Tara?" he asked, when they were headed to the elevator.

"What's up, sugar butt?"

"I can't believe you just called me that." Kerry gave her a wan smile.

"Okay. Yes, Kerry, what can I do for you?"

"How long have you known that Jericho was gay? Nobody in the room looked surprised. And I was shocked."

"You couldn't tell?"

"We don't have secret gay infrared or something." Which wasn't exactly true. Maybe Kerry just hadn't seen past the glitz. "No. I couldn't tell."

Tara shrugged. "I've always known. Outside of the public, he doesn't make much of a secret of it. If you go to an exclusive event with him? Let's just say… everyone knows."

"So he's not really in the closet?"

"Not really. Not in inside circles."

Wow. Kerry had no idea what to do with that information. "And he wanted to be out."

"Yeah. He always has. Just probably not in this exact circumstance."

Kerry couldn't imagine the horror of his brother or Robbie walking in on him if he was in… that situation. The idea of the whole world seeing it? Of the pictures being splashed all over the Internet, on every computer screen, talked about on the radio, on talk shows, on TMZ? Horrifying.

"This must be awful for him."

Tara squeezed his shoulder. "We're going to do our best to fix it, babe."

"Yeah. I know."

JERICHO was showered and dressed in a respectable pair of khakis, a T-shirt, and a cardigan when Tom's limo pulled into the driveway.

"Get in," Tom said.

Jericho got into the car. They rode toward the city in silence, like Tom was some parent who was letting him think about what he'd done. He sure as hell *was* thinking about it. He barely remembered that night, the bathroom, deciding it wasn't such a bad idea to have some stranger suck him off in public. It wasn't one of his more lucid decisions, and he'd been so angry at the closet, at George, at life. In less than three minutes, because, yeah, it had been that fast, he might have screwed up everything he'd worked toward for years.

"YOU want me to have a fiancé? Seriously? Nobody's going to agree to that." Jericho was pretty sure he was wrong. There had to be a ton of models looking for exposure who didn't mind being labeled as at least bisexual; there were probably actors too, but he didn't even want to think about that.

"We weren't going to go with someone in the industry. We need to sell the fairy tale—everyday, ordinary guy, you've been together for a long time, and you were protecting him. You love him; you were carried away in the moment. You know the story," George said.

"So some normal guy. Where are you going to find a normal guy who'll do this? He has to at least pass for the guy from the club."

"Small, dark hair, I don't think that will be a hard requirement to fulfill." George paused pointedly. "The job will be part-time, well paid, and short-term. There won't be any intimacy, other than the implied kind. It shouldn't even be a challenge to find *someone* to do it."

Jericho thought about it. He was out that way, out and proud and… in a fake long-term relationship, which wasn't ideal, but he could handle it. He could handle anything as long as they didn't shove him back in the closet, and it had an expiration date.

"And you think the public is going to love this kind of love story? It's not me with a pretty girl this time. Is this going to be a little too gay and a little too in their faces?"

"Maybe." George shrugged. "But what's our other option here, Jericho? Do you want this to be over? Because we can all quit right now, you can forget about your show, and I can hit the front nine before lunch. Is that what you want?"

"No," Jericho said quietly. "I want that role. I need that role." He was fucking tired of being paid to show up at crappy parties promoting products and the latest pop album. He wanted to *act*.

"Then we need to make you look as sympathetic as possible, and a long-term relationship with a regular guy is exactly the way to do that in this situation."

"Yeah. I agree." And Jericho did. Reluctantly.

"With dark hair and a slight build," George said.

"Yes." He remembered that much about the guy. Plus he'd seen the picture more times than he wanted to by the time Tom had come to get him.

"A guy who we can trust."

"Obviously."

George looked down toward the end of the table. "It's obvious who our choice should be. Kerry?"

Kerry, who'd been scribbling things down, looked up, surprised. "What?"

Chapter Four

"**WAIT.** Me?" Kerry stared at George and Abby. He got impassive stares in return. Kerry gave Tara a desperate look. She'd be on his side. Tara just shrugged as if to say, *well, it's not a bad choice*. Traitor. "Why on earth do you think I should do it? I'm not an actor."

He wasn't an actor, he wasn't interested in fame. He just wanted to do his job, get promoted, and not have to worry quite so much about money. He did *not* want to pretend he was in love with Jericho Knox. If he even could.

"That's the point. We don't *want* an actor, Kerry," George said gently. "We want someone we can trust. We can trust you, can't we?"

"What about the actual guy in the picture?" Kerry looked at Jericho. "Can't he do it?"

Jericho looked incredibly uncomfortable for a moment. And then he muttered, "I don't know his name, let alone where to find him."

"Not at all?"

Jericho winced. "You know how it is. You're at a club…." He only looked a little bit embarrassed by the fact.

Kerry most certainly did *not* know how that was. He'd never been a hot, famous guy. That kind of stuff didn't just happen to nobodies like him—he could count on zero fingers the times he'd walked into a club and had some stranger offer him sexual favors in some dark back room. He wasn't sure if he even wanted them to.

"So you have no idea who he is?"

"No."

"The love of Jericho's life could be anyone with dark hair, pale skin, and a slight build. And you think *I'm* the best candidate for the job?"

Everyone around the table nodded. Kerry felt sweat drip down his back. He wasn't meant to be in front of the cameras. He was the guy in the computer room tweeting and making schedules and phone calls. No. Absolutely not. He hadn't been in public much for the swarms of cameras and shouting that tended to follow their higher profile clients around, but he knew what it was like. He'd analyzed red-carpet video and airport paps, and damn if he could do that. He wasn't cut out for the spotlight.

"I can't act. I don't know how to pretend I'm in love when we're strangers. Nobody's going to buy it. There has to be someone else who's looking to get their name into the press. I'm not your guy."

"Kerry, you'll be perfect. You won't seem rehearsed. Jericho knows what he's doing. Plus, models are too tall to fit the profile. And the boy next door will seem so much more authentic."

Kerry looked over at Jericho in panic. He didn't want the guy to think he wasn't happy for the work or, like, repulsed by him, he just… he worked behind the scenes of publicity stunts and filled in the little details. He didn't *participate* in them.

"I'm going to use the bathroom," Jericho announced. He got up and headed toward the break room area.

"I really don't think I can do this," Kerry whispered as soon as Jericho was gone.

George gave him a long look. "It would really show us you're a team player, Kerry. You want to be a team player, don't you?"

Translated—do this or you'll never get a promotion. Don't do this and your days here are numbered. George would never make the threat outright, well, *probably* couldn't make the threat outright, but he sure as hell could insinuate like a champ. Kerry got the picture.

"Team player."

"Yes. Jericho's team. He needs you to get through this. He needs you to keep his role on *Steel Street* and stay relevant to the public. Jones & Keller needs popular stars like him on our roster. We *all* need you."

Kerry knew the silence was uncomfortable, deafening even, but he didn't want to agree. Of course he knew George, and he knew what was expected of him if he wanted to get ahead in his job. If he didn't want to end up on the couch, surfing the want ads for the next forever until he ended up with a job waiting tables.

"So if I do this, who can I tell?" Kerry asked. "I live with my brother. My parents will die if they think the guy in that picture is me. My brother would probably kill Jericho unless he knows the truth."

"You can tell him. Is he going to be a liability?"

"No, of course not. You can trust Cole, as long as he knows what's going down."

"He'll need to sign paperwork. So will you."

"Of course." There was no such thing as trust, no matter what they'd said a few minutes before. Kerry didn't blame them. He felt a little queasy. A lot queasy, actually.

Jericho came in and flopped back down on his seat.

"So… Kerry. Are you going to do this?"

"I would," Oscar said. "If Kerry isn't up to it. I can dye my hair."

Kerry saw Jericho sigh, like this whole thing was pissing him off. He was the one with his dick out on the Internet, though, even if most of it was hidden…. Kerry didn't get why he was so affronted. It wasn't like Kerry asked for any of this to happen. Far from it.

"No. It's okay," he said quietly. "I'll do it." He tried to ignore the heavy dread that settled hard somewhere around his chest and spread until it filled every crevice in his body.

"Remember, we're going to turn it around quickly. You'll be in love. You were violated. You've been together for a while."

"Hasn't Jericho been publicly dating?" Kerry asked. He didn't like where that was heading. Of course the public would assume they were just publicity dates after they figured out the truth. And he could always call them friends. There was an answer for everything in this damn business.

"Kerry, you're asking questions you know the answer to already."

"I know. I'm sorry. I do know the answer. I think I might need to take a breather. Do you mind if we take a quick break?"

"Yes. That's fine. But then we need to get back in here and get some strategies in place."

"Okay."

KERRY stood and stumbled out of the office. He made it into the elevator before he collapsed against the side of it.

Holy hell, what did I just get myself into?

He knew he didn't have a ton of choices. He knew, okay. He also knew it was probably going to suck. A lot. But it was only a few months, right? Until Jericho left for Vancouver and filming, and they could quietly fade away and release a back page statement months later about how they'd grown apart because of distance. Right? That's how Kerry would do it; all flash at the front but a whisper at the end. Might not make the most publicity, but that wasn't what Jericho needed. He needed respectability. He needed a sheen put onto a series of engineered mistakes and a holy hell of a mess. Kerry didn't know how he was going to manage to be that sheen.

Kerry got out of the elevator and walked through two huge, heavy, glass doors into the courtyard, where they had lunch sometimes when there was time and everyone had been organized enough to bring something. It was mostly in the shade with huge building walls surrounding it, but there was a small patch of sun on one of the middle tables, and Kerry happily sank into a chair right near it. The cushions were soft and warm; the air had a slight breeze, even within the courtyard. He concentrated on breathing in and out, in and out, and he wondered if the rest of the people in the office would notice if he never came back.

"Hey. You good?"

Kerry's eyes had been closed, so he jumped at the gravelly sound of a barely familiar voice. Jericho, of all people.

"Um. I'm sure you can guess the answer to that."

Jericho sat at the table and pulled out a pack of cigarettes. "You don't have to do this, you know."

"I didn't know you smoked."

"I don't, really. Just when I'm stressed."

Kerry snorted out a derisive laugh. "This has you stressed? I can't imagine how."

Jericho's sly smile was actually kind of beautiful. *Don't think that.* That was the last thing Kerry needed to think going into the whole mess.

"Just a little bit."

"And I do have to do it. You missed the very strong hint that if I don't do this I'm not a team player and I don't want my job. I'm not like you. I don't get to pick and choose my assignments by the ones that speak to me." He'd seen Jericho quoted as saying that before. Might as well remind him the world didn't work like that for most people.

"You don't know that I have that choice either."

"Well, then neither of us do. And I'd really like to not get fired if that's possible."

"Guys like that George dude are jackasses. Get a little bit of power, and they run people's lives without permission."

Kerry had the feeling they'd been running Jericho's for a while. At least until he rebelled and did something to change the entire game. "Yeah. Well, he runs mine."

"Fuck." Jericho closed his eyes and pushed on the sockets. "This is the last fucking thing I need, some long-term PR bullshit. I was supposed to spend the summer getting into my role. Not parading around an office assistant."

So Kerry and Jericho being on the same side had lasted about ten seconds. About what he expected, he guessed.

"Thanks a fucking lot," Kerry said. "You know, you're not exactly the way I planned to spend my summer either."

"Well, you could say no, quit here, and find another job. If I say no to this, I can kiss my career good-bye. No role, an even worse reputation. I'd be fucked and never hired again."

"Do you not grasp what would happen to me if I don't do my job? Jones & Keller might not be the only PR firm in town, but everyone has a phone. And e-mail. My career would be over too." Kerry was starting to see why Tara and Abby had said Jericho wasn't easy to deal with sometimes—looked like he saw everything from his own perspective, and screw everyone else. Pretty par for the course in this town. He remembered that Tara said the words asshole and self-involved. Seemed pretty damn accurate.

"Whatever," Jericho said.

"Anyway, what the hell difference does it make?" Kerry said. "If it wasn't me, it would be someone else. This is the best way we could come up with to get you out of this."

"Yeah, and whose idea was this whole scheme?"

Shit. "Mine."

"And you just happened to fit the profile?" Jericho asked. "Was that fake surprise in there? Oh, don't pick me. I don't want to be the one getting all the attention for once. Stop. Please." Jericho fake fanned himself. "Things are starting to be pretty clear."

"It wasn't like that at all. I don't want this. I—"

"Save it. I've known a million guys like you. Just took me a second to recognize the signs."

Kerry stood and pushed his chair back hard. "You really are the asshole everyone says you are," he barked. "I'll be upstairs. So much for my couple of minutes to calm down."

He didn't get anything but an eye roll from Jericho.

Kerry had thought the worst part was going to be what his parents thought, or his friends, or living it down once they "broke up." Oh hell no, that wasn't going to be it. The worst part, the worst part by far? That was going to be Jericho Knox himself. Asshole.

He punched the elevator button hard with his thumb and waited impatiently for it to come down. He smelled more than felt Jericho behind him, expensive cologne and a slight hint of cigarette. Kerry was determined not to say a word.

The elevator came, and he stepped in silently. He pushed the button for the fourth floor and stared at the wood-grain wall. He wasn't going to talk. Hell, no. It was hard to tamp down his nervous need to babble, but maybe the anger helped a little.

When they got to the fourth floor he stalked off the elevator and back to the conference room. Abby, Tara, Oscar, and George were waiting along with Jericho's agent, Tom.

"I'm ready to get started."

"Great," George said as soon as they all sat.

Jericho slumped into his chair. He looked sulky and only slightly beautiful. Jericho wouldn't look at him, or anyone else, just stared at the table and picked at a tiny hangnail he had on his ring finger. Kerry decided he was not a fan. Beautiful didn't mean anything when someone was a complete and utter ass.

"What should we start with?" George asked.

"Time limits," Kerry said decisively. "I'm going to need to know when this thing is supposed to be over. Exactly."

IT was insane how easily this table full of people who didn't really know him, sat there and planned the next few months of Jericho's *life* like it was no big deal.

"We'll want to have the couple seen out at the typical hotspots," Kerry said.

Kerry talked about the stunt like he wasn't involved, like it was some abstract thing in the third person. Jericho realized things must always be like that for them, not real people but pieces on a game board. He was like an objective, get him in the right places, get a certain number of pictures to a certain number of tabloids and websites, and the results would be optimal. Jericho wanted to walk away and never come back.

When he'd dreamed of being an actor when he was a kid, living in Hollywood and being someone important, he'd never thought he'd be in a boardroom having his personal life planned out like a script. It was naïve, sure, but he missed being that kid who had everything in front of him and didn't know he'd have to do a million underhanded fake things to get it.

"What? Are we going to arrange for another fake sex pic too? Maybe get a full shot of my dick this time?" Jericho grumbled.

"*No.*" Kerry mustn't have heard the sarcasm. "We want this to be wholesome and something that the public can like. We want them to like *you*. No dick pics."

"I wasn't serious." Jericho rolled his eyes.

"Oh. I knew that."

Kerry shuffled a stack of papers, and the silence in the room got thick and uncomfortable. Tara cleared her throat and pointed at a block on the apparent schedule of his new life, at least two weeks of it. "Where do you want to go for this dinner? It has to be high profile, but…."

Jericho stopped listening. He imagined her question was inane, more meant to save Kerry than to deal with any real detail of the plan.

Jericho had had enough of the meeting, which was a familiar sensation. He had to get out.

"Listen, can you guys hack out the rest of this on your own?"

He didn't even give the excuse of errands this time, just wanted to get the hell out of there. It felt like he couldn't breathe. He didn't want to look at his social media mentions. He didn't want to do anything… just wanted to go home and hide. Maybe swim for a little while, cave up in his media room and watch movies and not look at any single place where he and his scandal might be mentioned. The team was going to clean it up with tweets from him—if those hadn't been sent out already—with mentions of Kerry, love, and privacy, and whatever other bullshit spinning they'd planned. He didn't want any part of it. And to think he'd been attracted to Kerry. He wasn't any different from the rest of them. Probably worse, since he'd managed to wrangle himself into the spotlight and pretend it had nothing to do with him.

"Yeah. You can go, Jericho," George said.

Tom stood as well. "I'll drop you at home."

Jericho supposed Tom didn't want him seen catching a cab or something. Like he wasn't capable of arranging his own car service. Jericho didn't have the energy to argue. It felt like he was spinning in circles. He didn't know what to do, and the easiest thing to do was nothing.

He followed Tom out of the building and tried not to think about them planning his future like some war room scenario up there. They were doing him a favor. All of them. Jericho tried to remind himself of that. Sure, that Kerry guy was probably doing himself more of a favor than Jericho. And from what he'd heard already, Kerry was going to be moving into his house, the one place where he could be himself—play video games, swim, and not worry who was taking pictures of him. It was going to be invaded by the spin team and their fame-hungry little backroom grunt. Fine.

But he had at least the rest of day to himself, right? They weren't moving forward with the moving in part of the plan until it was dark outside and hard for photographers to see. If Kerry had supposedly been there for months, it would hardly do to have someone catch him moving in.

Jericho and Tom slid into the black car. Tom rolled down the window. "Jericho's place first, then my office. Thanks, Maurice," he said to the driver. Jericho heard some rustling—the driver must've been finishing his lunch—then the car started, and they slowly pulled out of the parking garage into the bright Los Angeles sun.

Jericho felt like it should be cloudy or something, to reflect the shit hole his life had turned into overnight.

"What are the chances this is actually going to work, Tom? Like, am I going through with this farce for nothing?"

Tom shook his head. "No. I actually outlined the plan to the studio, and they said it might just work. Don't get defeated. Remember, if Jones does his job right, we can erase the scandal and have the public seeing true love and only that in weeks. Days even."

"But gay true love. Didn't you guys always say that wouldn't get me any leading roles?"

"I guess we'll have to see about that. This is what we have to work with now, and we're going to do it, right? You're going to play your part with this Kerry boy and make it believable?"

"Of course. I want my role. I just… hope all this is worth it."

"It will be."

They fell silent again on the way back to Jericho's place. He had a lot to think about, and he supposed Tom did as well. Jericho wasn't his only client, just his most troublesome. He needed to get the guest room set up for his very unwanted guest, work out with his trainer, and go shopping, although he had a feeling he wouldn't be doing that for himself for a while, which was annoying. Grocery shopping was one of Jericho's simple pleasures. He figured he'd make himself a somewhat forbidden snack and watch two movies before he faced reality.

There were paps at his gate when he pulled up. He highly doubted George had sent them, not when he didn't have anything set up he wanted them to see. They were there trying to catch Jericho in his shame.

He dialed in the gate code on his phone, and the gate swung open. The driver took them through, and they let the gate close before Jericho got out.

"Thanks, Tom. I am sorry about this mess. It was the last thing I expected to happen."

"I know, Jay. We'll sort this out. I'll be on the phone the rest of the day with the studios and the director. We're going to make sure you have your part. You'll be on a plane come September, I promise."

"Thanks."

He patted Tom on the shoulder and hopped out of the car. Made sure to make it into the house before the driver backed up and the gate opened once again.

Chapter Five

"HEY, man," Kerry said when he walked in the door. He was glad it was just Cole in the apartment. They had some things to talk about, and Robbie didn't need to get involved in them.

"What's up, Bro?" Cole paused his video game and tossed the controller onto their thrift shop coffee table. It always felt weird for Kerry to come home to their very humble apartment after a day dealing with the rich and fabulous in a very expensive office. Mostly a relief, to tell the truth. He plunked down the box of papers he'd brought with him along with the two suitcases he'd dragged up from their basement storage locker.

"I've got something to talk to you about."

"That doesn't sound good. You're not moving out, are you?" Cole eyed the suitcases.

"No. Well, sort of, but not really. It's just temporary."

"What?" Cole shot out of the slouchy position he'd been in, his spine ramrod straight. Cole had chosen specifically to live in an apartment instead of the dorms or the frat house because he wanted to live with family. He'd always been that guy. They both were.

"I'm not moving out," Kerry promised. "I just have to go stay somewhere else for a while."

"Where?"

"Let me start at the beginning."

Kerry took a deep breath, which was mostly just pausing. Or stalling. He had serious doubts Cole was going to be okay with what he was about to do. Hell, he had serious doubts that he was okay with it. But it was part of the job. Right?

"I'm waiting." Cole didn't look like he was waiting… more like he was deciding how pissed he was about to be.

"So, you know how we deal with celebrities and publicity, right?"

"Yes. Because you work for a publicist. I am in college, Kerry, not kindergarten."

"Okay. Sorry. Anyway, one of our clients has gotten himself into a bit of trouble lately."

"Which one?"

Technically he wasn't supposed to say much, but he'd gotten a pass for Cole; well, that, and a huge NDA for him to sign, but he'd get to that part later. "Jericho Knox."

Cole's eyes flew open. "You work for him directly?"

"Yeah. I do now. I think you can guess why."

"Man, he's in shit for that picture. It's all anyone on campus is talking about."

"Well, the company has come up with a plan to turn that around, make people talk about some good things."

"What's the plan?"

Cole knew. He knew the plan was going to involve Kerry somehow, and he wasn't going to like it. Kerry could see it in his face.

"They decided Jericho needs to have a serious partner nobody knew about who could've been the guy in that picture. A fiancé. One who is slight… and has dark hair… someone they could trust who wouldn't blab to the tabloids and screw up the story. They want it to look like a serious couple who had their privacy invaded."

Cole froze. "Don't even say it, Bro. You're not doing this."

"I am. It's going to be me. I'm Jericho Knox's new fiancé."

"No. Hell no. My brother isn't going to be all over the fucking Internet as the guy who blew Jericho Knox in public. You didn't, did you?"

"Screw you. Of course it's not me. I've met the guy twice, and I didn't exactly like him. Plus, it was in a boardroom, not a bar."

"Okay. Just making sure. I don't like this. I don't want that for you."

"They're going to spin it, blame the person who took the picture for abusing our private moment. As of tomorrow, Jericho Knox and I are going to be in love. And engaged to be married. Engaged people have sex. People will… forget about the picture eventually."

"Fucking hell, man...." Cole just sank into the couch like the shock was too much for his stomach muscles to handle. "And you have to move in with him?"

"Yeah. There are paps camped out in front of his house trying to get a reaction out of him. And even if there weren't, Jones would hire some to make sure I was seen there. It's going to have to look pretty realistic to turn things around for Jericho. A hell of a lot more realistic than the typical celebs who go on a few dates with their assistants in the background and get their picture taken by some fans."

"I don't even get your world." Cole shook his head. He looked disgusted.

"Sometimes I don't either."

"So you're moving in with Jericho fucking Knox."

"You make him sound like a monster."

"Is he any better? From what I've seen, the guy's an asshole. And... wasn't he supposed to be some kind of womanizer?"

"He's not. I asked. He's not even bi. That was all just spin to keep his name in the tabloids, and the public away from the truth."

"Gay Camouflage 101?" Cole asked.

Kerry shrugged. "Yeah. Pretty common move. I can't believe I was surprised when I found out the truth."

"Fuck."

"Anyway, you can't tell the guys. I mean, Robbie yeah, since he knew last week that I'd never met Jericho, so he'd have to know something was up, but nobody else. Or Mom and Dad."

"What the hell, K? They're not going to believe you just miraculously started dating a movie star, didn't tell them, and got engaged. Nobody's going to buy it."

"I'm going to make them buy it. That's my job. Your only job is to not tell them the truth. It would get too messy if a ton of people know." Kerry felt a disgusting pit in his stomach. He had a feeling his parents were going to end up with the truth and a whole lot of promises not to say anything.

Cole glared at him. "Just in case you were wondering, I really don't like this. I doubt you were wondering, though."

"I think you made that clear. I don't want to lose my job, man. They didn't actually say that, because I'm pretty sure that would be unethical if not illegal, but I also don't think they'd make it easy for me to keep my job if I don't do this. And technically? This is my job. To make Jericho Knox look like a nice guy."

"Instead of some dude who got sucked off in a club."

"Hey. Sex isn't a bad thing. A sex picture on the Internet when you have a new role on *Steel Street* kind of is. That's what this is all about."

"He's going to be on *Steel Street*? Awesome gig. Season one was badass."

Kerry cringed. Usually he was so good at holding his tongue around Cole and Robbie. "I know. And I really shouldn't have told you that either. It's contingent on this working out. They don't want damaged goods on a prime-time big network show."

"Yeah, I can imagine. Jesus."

"Seriously. Tell nobody. No one. I'm going to have to make you sign some papers to say you won't talk, and I can't help you if you get in trouble. I don't have the power or the money."

"I won't, man. I'm not stupid. Besides, how long did I know you were gay before anyone else did?" At least three years. Cole had a point.

"I know. Sorry, I'm just freaking out. So, I wanted you to know. They're sending a car over for me later tonight, and it's going to get a little weird."

"No kidding."

"Just, Cole?"

"Yeah?"

Kerry squeezed his eyes shut for a long moment. The next few months were going to be so hard for his family, and he couldn't believe what he was about to put them through. "Remember. Whatever you read about me in the tabloids isn't true. None of it will be. Half the time, it'll be my team telling the magazines what to say to get the most out of the situation. Hell, it might even be me writing the press releases. They're going to be crap, I just want you to be ready for it. Okay?"

"Yeah. None of it will be true. Got it."

"Thank you. I'm really sorry about this. I hope it's over with soon and we can just... forget it ever happened."

"Me too, Bro. I love you, man. Sorry you have to do this."

IT wasn't that long of a drive home to Oxnard, and he had the whole afternoon and early evening. Kerry figured he at least owed it to his parents to warn them, even if he wasn't supposed to tell them the whole truth. The story was going to hit early in the morning, and he wanted them to at least be prepared. It wasn't a conversation to have over the phone. He'd told his mom he was on his way and had Cole with him for a visit. Cole had been distinctly against lying to them about the relationship. Kerry figured if anyone knew how to keep their mouths shut, it was his family. He'd already decided he was going to do his best to obey the letter of the law but give them as much information as he could.

It was lunchtime when they pulled up to the house he and Cole had grown up in. It was spacious and friendly, and not too far from the beach. Sometimes Kerry was tempted to move back home, live in a decent place, and get an easier job. Los Angeles was exhausting after a while. But he didn't know what he'd want to do with his life if it wasn't what he was doing. He'd have to start all over. He supposed he'd at least wait until Cole was out of school and settled in a job to think about his future plans.

Their parents were waiting for them when they arrived. Kerry and Cole hadn't been there since Easter—both had been insanely busy with school and work and commitments. It felt like forever.

Kerry and Cole both hugged their parents tight and followed them into the house.

"I made lunch, guys," Mom said. "Grilled cheese and tomato soup." She was still wearing her walking clothes from earlier in the day and had her hair, dark like theirs but streaked with gray, up in a high ponytail.

"That sounds great, Mom. How's your week been?" They might not visit as often as they'd like, but Cole and Kerry talked to their parents nearly every day. Their family had always been close. Tight. It was the way things were done.

"I've been working on the MG," their dad said. "I think I'm going to have it running soon." Their dad's favorite weekend activity was fixing up old British cars. Cole usually puttered around the garage with him when he was home. Kerry had never had much interest in his car, other than if it got him places and didn't break down.

"You'll have to show me what you did," Cole said with a grin. "Well, after."

Their parents both turned to glance at Kerry. He might have warned them that he had some news.

"Are you okay, Ker?" their dad asked. Both Mike and Susan Pickering were the type who got to the point. Quickly.

"Sort of."

"You didn't get into any trouble, did you?"

He took a deep breath. "No. Not exactly."

"You might as well just tell us. Save all of us from whatever it is you're putting yourself through right now." Their mom reached out and put her hands over his.

"So, there are going to be some stories coming out about me tomorrow. In the tabloids, probably the entertainment news."

"What?" That was obviously not what they'd expected to hear. How could it be? Kerry made a quick decision. Letter of the law wasn't happening. He couldn't do that to his family. They were getting the whole story.

"Yeah… um, they're not exactly true."

His mom gave him a long, questioning look. Kerry knew she'd never been a fan of his job. She was going to be a hell of a lot less of one after what he was about to tell her.

"What are these stories going to say?"

"First, I need you to promise me you're not going to say anything, okay? I had to sign a nondisclosure form, and I could get in serious trouble if this got out. Cole signed one too before we got in the car to come here. I'm not even supposed to tell you guys, but I'm going to anyway. No matter what anyone says to you about me, this stays in this room, okay?"

It really was better that way. His parents had to be involved. They would've flipped out if they weren't. He'd talk to George about it on Monday. Hopefully he'd be okay with the situation.

"Yes," their mom said.

"Of course," their dad echoed.

"Seriously. No matter what. I could get sued. Fired. Just… don't tell anyone the truth."

"The truth about what, Kerry."

"I'm not really engaged to Jericho Knox."

Their mom made a face. "I should hope not," she said. "He's been all over the—" She looked at Kerry's dark hair and small shoulders. Kerry figured out when she put two and two together. "They're going to say you were the man in the picture, aren't they? That's not you, is it?"

"Jesus. Cole asked me that too. No. I met Jericho in a boardroom. We barely know each other. That's *not* me." He made a face. "What do you guys think I do in LA?"

"I'm not judging, dear. I just wanted all the facts."

His dad didn't say anything, but he looked angry. Kerry figured he'd better keep talking. He hated explaining the PR game to people who weren't in it. It always sounded so slimy. Probably because a lot of the time it was. "They need to clear his image up. He was offered a great part on a TV series, but they'll drop him if he doesn't fix this."

"So they're going to say he's engaged? To you?"

"Yeah, and our privacy was violated." Kerry shrugged. "It's one thing if it's an anonymous hookup in a club bathroom. It's another if it's between long-term partners who got carried away in the moment. They won't fire him for being gay, that day has passed. But they would fire him for getting, well, you've seen the picture. Our team is trying to turn that around, make people forget the scandal and fall in love with his relationship."

"The relationship that doesn't exist."

"And they want you to do it?" His father was still scowling.

"They wanted someone they could trust who fit the general look of the man in the picture. So yeah. Me. Also they wanted an everyday guy. That Hollywood fantasy of marrying the celebrity makes this all seem a lot more glamorous, I guess. I fit the bill, and I was sitting right in front of them."

"Baby, you know what I'm going to say," his mom told him.

"Yeah. I know." Of course he knew. He'd say it to anyone he loved as well. He knew. But it was too late to change his mind. Papers were signed, and his future was on the line, ethical or not.

"Believe me, I already said it," Cole grumbled.

"And I'm guessing you wouldn't do this if you didn't have to."

"They kind of implied that I wasn't a team player if I didn't. It was all implications of course. They'll always cover their asses, but the message was if I chose not to participate, the results wouldn't be good for my future."

"Barbaric." He knew by the mom claws, and his father's disapproving face, and how Cole gripped the table that his family wasn't happy, and they had every right to be angry. He would be if one of them was in his place.

"Mom, it's just show business. It's always like that for everyone."

"But you're not in show business."

"I guess I am now." Kerry shrugged.

"Sweetheart. You can quit, you know. Start over. This isn't you."

And that was exactly what he was worried about. Kerry didn't have the will to start his life over. At least not yet. He didn't even know how he'd do it. So he would go through with this and take stock afterward. Maybe it wouldn't be that bad.

They sat there quietly for a long time, talking as a family. Kerry gave his parents and his brother things they could say if people asked questions, did his job and trained them just like he'd train any other client in what to say… that was if he'd ever been let out of the office long enough to do it. His first big PR job. And it was the size of a whale. His old desk and collection of Twitter accounts was starting to sound awfully nice.

JERICHO knew Kerry was supposed to be there by now. They'd planned for him to drive in around nine, come straight through the gates, and park his car alongside the house. The photographers had given up for the day, since Jericho wasn't giving them anything, and the ones who they'd hired to come see him and Kerry in their happy relationship weren't going to be there until the news hit the tabloids in the morning. It would give him a few moments to get psyched up for the role he hadn't known he'd be playing.

Fiancé.

Intimate, sweet, loving. It wasn't something that came easy to him, but he was an actor, damn it, and a better one than he got credit for. He'd make it work, and he'd make it believable. He finished getting the guest room ready—he hadn't done it when he first meant to and forgot to ask Debbie to do it when she was there earlier. Then he grabbed a beer and flopped down on the leather couch in the living room he barely used to wait for his new roommate to arrive. It was warm out, and Jericho had all the sliding doors and windows thrown open. He loved the city in the late spring before it hit astronomical heat and he had to turn on the air-conditioning inside. Instead he leaned back and closed his eyes and enjoyed the last moments of warm, comfortable night air before George's minion invaded his one quiet space.

As expected, Jericho soon heard a knock on the door. Kerry the minion had thankfully remembered the gate code Jericho had given him, so that part wasn't screwed up. And here he was. Jericho hauled himself off the couch, took another swig of his beer, and set it down on a coffee table that his decorator would probably kill him for setting sweating beer on. He ambled to the door, each step slower than the last, and opened it.

Kerry was standing on the other side, cute and preppy as always, and Jericho hated that he was a little attracted to the guy who was orchestrating this whole farce, but he so was. Probably more than a little. Kerry looked like a college kid standing there with his suitcase, duffel bag, T-shirt, and cargo shorts. Jericho had no idea how old he was. He hadn't thought to ask.

"You are, like, over twenty-one, aren't you?"

Kerry managed to look offended. "I'm twenty-five. So yes. I'm legal."

"Come in." Jericho knew it sounded about as welcoming as a frost storm, but what was he supposed to do? Say yes, please come in and take over my life more than you and your people already have?

Even if he's using you he's still doing you a favor....

Still, Jericho felt a little bitter having George's world inside his own.

"Um, where should I put this stuff?"

"Come on, guest room's down this way."

Jericho stopped by the coffee table and grabbed his beer.

"Do you think you should be drinking, you know, after last time?" Kerry said. Then he blushed, bit his lip, and looked like he wished he'd done anything else.

"You don't get to tell me what to do when we're in here. I don't want you here. It's just for appearances, okay?"

"Hey, don't act like this is some vacation for me."

"Isn't it?" Jericho sneered. "I'd imagine wherever you live doesn't look like this. Must've crossed your mind when you were setting up this whole charade."

"You're right. My apartment isn't glamorous like this place. But it's also a hell of a lot friendlier."

"Come this way. Your room is at the end of this hallway. There's an adjoining bathroom, so you'll just be able to set all your stuff up for however long you need to stay here."

"Thanks." Kerry sounded like thanking him was the last thing he wanted to do. He ran fingers through his dark floppy hair, and Jericho felt his belly heat. He had to admit that at least on the surface, Kerry was a perfect pick. He looked a hell of a lot like the guy in the picture from behind, and he was the exact kind of guy Jericho would try to meet if they were out in a club.

He wished he didn't hate their methods as much as he did. He opened the door to the guest room. "Here you go. I'm going to go out and swim for a while, so, like, just do whatever it is you do at home, I guess."

Jericho had zero intentions of inviting Kerry to use the pool with him. It was the last of his sanctuary, and he didn't want to share it. Not that day at least. He wasn't a total asshole, but he wanted one more night alone in the water. He was already in trunks and flip-flops, so he stripped off his shirt and strolled out to the patio. It was warm and quiet outside. He couldn't hear the noise of the city in the distance or the sounds of Kerry settling into Jericho's life. He slid off his shoes and waded down the stairs into the shallow end of the pool.

Jericho had always liked how pools lit up at night, how the water turned that unearthly glowing green color and it almost seemed like when he splashed it in the air, it would turn into little jewels.

He swam back and forth for a long time. The quiet helped him think, which probably wasn't the best thing in his situation. But it did clear his mind. By the time he got out of the pool, he felt a little better somehow.

Not about the situation, since it was still a huge mess, but better.

He dried off and slipped his flip-flops back on. He slid his shorts off and wrapped the towel tightly around his hips. Then Jericho flopped onto one of his huge deck loungers and hid from the world some more. Or at least one adorable, social-climbing, annoying PR minion.

Chapter Six

THE first thing Kerry did in his new room was put away his clothes. He'd never liked a mess, and it seemed disrespectful somehow to leave a mess in someone else's home. Then he didn't quite know what to do. He decided he'd make himself at least a little bit familiar with the place. As far as he knew, Jericho was still sulking out by the pool, so Kerry had a run of the house. The lights were all on, and they seemed to make the whole interior glow. The main part of the house was one huge room—kitchen with hanging copper pots that he doubted Jericho ever used, a thick island, then an enormous living room area, a dining room off to the side, and the fireplace that rose two stories up to the ceiling. The stairway to the second story, where Jericho's suite was, circled up, wrought iron and intricate. Above them was a landing and apparently the rest of the areas that were off-limits. At least according to his surly new roommate. He knew if he went down the stairs by the kitchen, he'd find a basement gym and pool hall. Supposedly a movie room as well, which must have gotten use because there wasn't a television to be found in the main area.

The living room was pretty self-explanatory, mostly art and expensive-looking leather furniture, but Kerry decided he'd get acquainted with the kitchen. He was going to have to get some groceries, which hopefully would be pretty easy. He wasn't Jericho-status by any means; he'd just had his "face" plastered on a bunch of tabloids that most people didn't read. He could go to the store. It'd be fine. Right. He was a little hungry, though. The nerves had hit him earlier, and he hadn't had much of anything to eat. So he decided to make himself something. Thing was, the food wasn't his. And he felt awkward.

Shit. I have to talk to him.

He went out to the pool, where he found Jericho with his feet dipped in.

"Hey, um, I was going to make some scrambled eggs. Do you want any?"

"No."

"Is it cool if I use your kitchen?"

Jericho rolled his eyes. "No, you have to make them on the barbecue outside."

"Just checking."

"Whatever. I think I'm going to go out."

"You probably shouldn't do that." It was weird being part of the PR stunt and knowing exactly how to run one at the same time.

"I shouldn't do what? Go have some fun?"

"No. Having fun was exactly what got us here in the first place, Jericho."

"Don't be condescending like that. You know, I never even fucking asked. Are you gay?"

Kerry cleared his throat. *Well, that's awkward.* "Yeah. Of course. I mean… how did you think they were going to explain us if I was straight?"

"I don't know. I tried not to think about it. Or you."

Nice. Jericho hadn't been nearly so bad when they'd been outside in the courtyard earlier. Kerry figured he was in for a long, long summer.

"Okay. Well, I'm going to go make eggs. Then I think I'm going to do some work on my computer. Please don't go out."

"Yeah. Fine."

After the chill of Jericho's reception outside, the kitchen was refreshingly silent. And empty. Jericho didn't seem to feel any inclination to come inside, so Kerry gathered his ingredients—eggs, a bit of cheddar, butter, chives—and then got to making dinner. After he cooked, he realized his stomach was a bit upset, maybe from being hungry, maybe from being stuck in the most luxurious place he'd ever been and hating every second of it. Who knew? He washed the pan when he was done and took the bowl with his eggs and a fork, plus a bottle of cranberry juice that he'd found, and padded back to his bedroom. Maybe he'd watch a few episodes of something on Netflix. He was nearly permanently behind on every show. He had to go to work the next day, and they were going to do their first date in the afternoon, which, *ugh.*

Kerry slid into his bed. It was too soft, too comfortable. He almost missed his lumpy, weird mattress from home. He flicked open his laptop and put in the Wi-Fi password Jericho had written on a card of info that he'd left on the bed. TV was perfect—the more mindless the better. He decided to take a leaf out of Jericho's book and try not to think about it. He'd survive this. He had to.

KERRY hadn't ever been in the back of a town car before. He hated to even call it a limo because it was more understated than that—just a big dark car with smoked windows and luxurious leather. Very celebrity, very upscale. He was also *very* uncomfortable. His first night with Jericho had been long and silent. He wasn't excited for another. He also wasn't excited for their first public date, the date that had already technically started.

"Where are we going, again?" Jericho asked.

Kerry and Tara had come up with a general plan, a story arc of their romance, as it were. They were supposed to already be close, close enough to be engaged, so the dates had to be casual, familiar, things people did together when they'd been a couple for a long time and finally decided to show their face in public. They'd decided to start easy.

"Just getting some frozen yogurt and shopping."

"Really?" Jericho made a honking noise. "Could you get any more generic? That's almost like a siren with a flag saying PR couple. I thought we were supposed to be selling this as genuine."

"We want your fans to see us, though. Fans of your old show, and then we'll work on the *Steel Street* demographic."

"Are all the fans of my old shows girls in Uggs and yoga pants? Because that's who goes to get frozen yogurt."

That was not stereotyping or anything. But the guy had a point. Sort of.

"Actually...." Kerry shrugged. "Kind of."

"Oh." Jericho looked a little annoyed to be the man candy to a bunch of millennial females. Kerry bit his tongue, but he wanted to remind the ass who paid for his house.

"What are we doing afterward?"

Cringe. Seriously. Kerry didn't even want to say it out loud.

"Tara thought it would be a good idea if we did a little shopping. Hit a few stores, buy some T-shirts or something. Public, casual, familiar."

"Fuck."

"You should probably work on your mouth. You don't want to swear in front of the fans."

"Are you goddamn serious? That's not going to happen."

Kerry sighed. "I'm not here to police you. I'm just trying to get the job done." He was annoyed, and it hadn't even been five minutes. "You don't have to love the date. You just have to sell it. Do you think you can do that?"

"Yeah. If there's anything I can do, it's sell it."

Fantastic. Could he have done that without the attitude? Kerry was amazed by how quickly he got over Jericho's magnificent presence and gorgeous face and moved on to being annoyed as hell.

"So we're going to park around the back of the shop and walk in, make it look nice and natural. Grab some yogurt, wander around the shopping area. Shouldn't be a problem."

"Yeah. No problems." Jericho slumped back in his seat like he always seemed to when he was irritated. Or unhappy. Or tired. Or hungover. Or just being Jericho. So far he'd done a lot of all of those things, and they all looked pretty much the same. Kerry looked out the window. He had a feeling he'd be doing a lot of looking out the window as long as he and Jericho were doing their thing. He wasn't exactly with the conversationalist of the century.

They pulled into the lot where their town car would wait for the signal to come pick them up.

"Showtime," Jericho said with a sigh.

"Yes. It's showtime."

He got out of the car, and Jericho hopped out on the other side and came around. Kerry was surprised when Jericho grabbed his hand, slid their fingers together, and gave him a dazzling smile.

"Ready to get this fucking thing over with?" he murmured through his teeth. He managed to keep the smile, which was pretty impressive.

"I suppose so."

IF there was something Kerry didn't think he'd ever be prepared for, it was the wall of paparazzi that someone had called in to greet them—most likely Abby. It felt like being an animal at a zoo; probably not the most original comparison in the world, but Kerry couldn't think of anything else once he was on the receiving end of a ton of googly-eyed flashing lenses.

Jericho let go of his hand, smiled down at him, and wrapped a muscular arm around his shoulder. He pulled

Kerry in and, under the guise of brushing a kiss in his hair, whispered, "Smile. You look terrified."

Kerry looked up at him, and, well, the look Jericho was giving him—sweet and happy and intimate—he couldn't help responding to it. So he smiled back and cuddled a little closer. The paps were shouting things at them. Things about the picture, about their sexuality, asking Jericho when they were going to get married. Kerry tried not to even look at them. He kept his focus on Jericho, who just smiled politely at them, which probably hurt his pride more than anything, and said nothing. By the time they'd gone ten feet, it felt like he'd been through a battle. By the time they got to the yogurt shop, he thought he was going to scream.

They strolled into the shop as planned. Jericho removed his arm but slid his hand down Kerry's arm until their fingers linked together. Kerry tried not to shake. *Get it done. You can do this.*

"What do you want, babe?" Jericho asked. The girls behind the counter were obviously trying to keep their cool, but Kerry had kind of forgotten what a big deal Jericho was over the past two days of being mostly annoyed with him. And he was. A big deal.

"I'll get the birthday cake flavor with cherries and mocha, please."

"And chocolate with brownie chunks for me." Jericho grinned at the girls. Kerry heard a few camera phones go off. Good. That's exactly what they wanted.

Maybe this whole damn thing would work, after all.

IT wasn't hard, not really. Jericho thought that maybe it should've been harder to sling his arm over Kerry's shoulder and act like they'd been together for years. It was actually a little… refreshing to finally have a guy by his side. Not that he'd tell Kerry that, of course. Sure, it was as fake as all the other bullshit they had him do, but maybe that hint of reality, that little bit of his own self that got to come out by holding hands and flirting with a man for once, instead of a sweet-smelling but oh so wrong woman, well that changed things. They took their yogurts and walked out of the store to sit at one of the outdoor picnic tables. Which was exactly what Jericho would do on a normal day. Eye roll.

Kerry flinched a little when the cameras started going off again.

"Be cool," Jericho leaned over and whispered. Then he brushed a short kiss across Kerry's forehead. Kerry looked up, and Jericho tried to give him his softest, most reassuring look. After all, this dumb show was worth nothing if Kerry couldn't pull it off. Jericho tried not to notice how soft his lips looked, or how he really seemed to trust Jericho in a sea of flashes and noise.

"Hey. Does Knox pay you to suck him off?"

Kerry flinched again. Harder this time, and Jericho pulled him close.

"I thought your people called these guys in," he whispered into Kerry's hair. "Why's that one being an asshole?"

"I thought we called them in too. I don't know what that guy's problem is. Just ignore him."

Jericho chuckled into Kerry's hair. "No kidding. Thanks for the pro tip."

Kerry actually managed to give him the perfect near-spouse look—a little exasperated, intimate, and with the hint of a smile.

There. Get a picture of that, douchewads.

"Ready to eat yogurt with the preteens?" Jericho asked.

"Yes. Then shopping and lunch, because I'm starving for real food, not whipped low-fat sugar."

"Didn't you eat this morning?" Jericho asked.

"Nah. I haven't had time to go to the store yet."

"There's food in my refrigerator."

Kerry gave him another look; this one wasn't quite so intimate. "That's your stuff. I'm not going to eat your food. I know I did last night, but I was going to replace the eggs when I had time."

Jericho rolled his eyes. "I think I can handle the strain on my food budget. Besides, you're not going to want to go to the store for the next few weeks. Not until your face is off the checkout line tabloids. Trust me."

He saw the moment Kerry realized exactly why. "Damn," he muttered. Sometimes Kerry forgot that most of America thought he was the guy on his knees in that picture. Jericho had no idea how Kerry forgot it, but he'd managed to.

"Just make me a list of what you like to eat. I'll add your stuff to my order. I'm also not going to the store anytime soon."

He slid his hand down the center of Kerry's back possessively. The single picnic bench meant they could get nice and close. They'd planned it strategically for a busy time so that plenty of teen girls with their nimble cell phone fingers would take pictures of them to post on the Internet. It'd look genuine. Organic. Promo gold right there, coursing over the Internet. They looked just like a couple.

"Relax," Jericho said again. He hoped he wouldn't have to keep repeating that to Kerry over and over.

Kerry melted up against him and covered Jericho's hand with his own.

"There ya go."

They sat, unnaturally close to each other on a rather visible table close to the sidewalk. "This looks so PR stunt-y," Jericho whispered. He couldn't believe Kerry and the others couldn't come up with a less cliché first date.

"I know. Our hope is people know the pictures are staged, but they think we're not—that we just wanted to show everyone who we are in a public place and get it out there."

"That's… a little convoluted for George," Jericho said. He smiled at Kerry for the cameras and forgot for a second that he kind of resented him.

"It is. But George isn't really in charge of this one. I am." Kerry shrugged. "We had to go somewhere cheap and accessible. Your new show has an adult audience, but your current fans are mostly young girls, like you said, and those girls in there will spread our picture everywhere. As long as we're somewhere they can see us."

"Yeah. I know that. But that was literally the first and last time I will ever be seen at fucking Pinkberry, okay?"

Kerry snorted. "Okay. We'll go for somewhere less yoga-pantsy next time."

"Where's lunch?" Jericho asked.

"The Ivy?"

Jericho laughed out loud. "Oh my *God*."

"I know, I know. But we might as well get it over with, right? Get a big batch of pictures out there and start setting the stage."

"Shhhh," Jericho said. "Remember people actually care what you say now. They're listening to you."

"Sorry." Kerry still had some lessons to learn about being on the other side of the equation.

They finished their yogurt and wandered through a few of the shops and then back to the waiting car.

"To the Ivy, the most obvious place in Los Angeles, then?"

"Yes. To the Ivy."

KERRY was relieved when they slid into the relative silence of the car after a long picture-filled lunch. He heard the paps outside still and Jericho's fan girls—hell, a hurricane would probably be quieter—but at least they were muffled down to a dull roar. Someone banged on the window of the car.

"Jesus," Kerry muttered.

Jericho didn't say anything. It was a big change from the attentive, loving, touchy-feely boyfriend he'd been only minutes before. Kerry got it, he knew what acting was, but damn it was a bit like whiplash. Jericho moved to the other side of the seat and pulled a water bottle from the back flap of the seat in front of him. Kerry figured he'd have to get all the way out of his seat to even reach his own water. Sometimes he hated tall people.

"You can have it, you know. It's just going to sit there until someone drinks it."

Kerry didn't answer him, but he did take his seatbelt off and reach for the water.

There was shitty traffic all the way to the office from the restaurant, which wasn't exactly a surprise. It seemed like getting everywhere in the back of Jericho's luxury car service took twice as long as it did when Kerry was driving himself.

"Don't you ever drive anywhere on your own?" Kerry asked. He was starting to feel a little bitchy. He hadn't ever been someone who handled being tired well.

So far that day, they'd had a handler from his agent's office, Jericho's agent, the driver, his security guard, the paparazzi, and about a crap ton of fans who'd probably been shipped in by Tara—or at least heavily tipped off—as certified witnesses to their adorable date. It was goddamn exhausting. Even though they were almost alone in the car, there was still a driver, stoic and professional though he was. Kerry wanted to go into his own room, shut the door, and not look at anyone for a good ten hours. He wasn't going to be that lucky.

"Didn't think you'd want to ride on the back of my Harley." Jericho smirked at him. He looked like he was getting pleasure out of being annoying. Which was also not exactly a shock.

Right. He knew Jericho had a motorcycle. Of course he did. What was that word again? Cliché.

"Right."

They fell into silence again after that, a bit more comfortable than the one on the way to the restaurant but still not exactly pleasant. It was nearly forty minutes later when they finally pulled into the back entrance of the office. They had a way for celebs to get in so people didn't see them coming and going through the main elevators. Kerry hadn't used it before. He felt like Batman going into the Batcave. He smiled a little at the thought.

"You like this, don't you?" Jericho asked.

"What?" Kerry didn't expect questions. He didn't expect them to speak since they'd only spoken once in the last forty minutes.

"You like how it feels to roll into the special lot in a big expensive car. You want to feel important."

Kerry shook his head. He wasn't sure he even felt like giving Jericho an answer. "We've been over this. You know why I'm doing it," Kerry said. "Do you listen to anything I say?"

"Right. You're doing it for the team." Jericho rolled his eyes.

"What the hell do you think I'm getting out of this? Sure, my pay during this mess is a hell of a lot better than it usually is, but I'm starting to wonder if it's worth it."

"Right again. And then when this is over and you get a part on some reality show, biggest celebrity ex-boyfriends do battle or some shit, and your name is all over the tabloids for fifteen minutes, it won't seem worth it at all."

"What the hell are you talking about? I want nothing to do with any of that stuff. I'm doing my job. End of story. *God*, you're unpleasant."

It had only been a day, and Kerry already hated seeing his name in the press. He didn't want to think about what his friends from home were probably thinking of him, or what Cole's friends on campus were saying to him. Kerry *hated* it, and if he wasn't fairly sure it would be the death of his career, he'd have already pulled out and told Jericho Knox to shove it up his perfectly toned and tanned ass.

"Good. Remind yourself of that when I'm all over you in public, and you're tempted to like it."

Kerry wanted to hit him.

He also sort of wanted to cry.

How the hell could that asshole tell that it was almost nice to bask in the Jericho sunlight, even if was all an act that he mostly hated? How could Jericho tell that Kerry had forgotten for a second that Jericho hated him when he smiled like they were in love? It hurt to have that accusation hurled at him, a little like a broken shard of glass rubbed into his skin.

"Don't worry. It's not going to be a problem." Kerry scowled and got out of the car. He didn't want to even ride in the super-secret celeb elevator with Jericho. He'd had enough for the day, and they still had to spend the whole night at his goddamn house. He was playing with the idea of having Tara set them up for more events so at least he could go somewhere. It was silent in that place, with Jericho basically refusing to talk to him. He felt like he was going insane.

Tara was waiting at the fourth floor for them.

"Hey, babe," she said. She gave Kerry a big hug. He'd actually missed her the past couple of days. Missed her expensive perfume that somehow still smelled like innocence and candy, missed her big smile and her hugs and her laughter.

"Hey," he said quietly.

"Are you okay?" she asked. She must've seen it in his face.

"I'll be fucking fantastic when summer is over," he muttered. "I can't stand him."

Tara's eyes widened. Great. Jericho must've heard that. What did he expect acting like the world's biggest douche? For Kerry to fall at his feet?

"Well," Tara said with a wince. "You might want to bottle up that rage because the public loved you two. I mean there was the usual homophobic assholes and a few jealous bitches, but in general, the overall response has been the best we've ever gotten."

"Really?" Kerry was actually only partly surprised. Chemistry was chemistry, even if it was heated annoyance covered by the sheen of attraction.

"Yeah. Even I was fooled. You guys looked adorable out there. Bravo."

"So, what does that mean?"

"It means we're going to ramp you up a little. There's another event in a couple of days. I think we're going to have you guys do a romantic little smooch on the red carpet."

Kerry choked. And he probably choked because his heart started pounding like a kettledrum at the thought of it. Kissing… kissing was so not part of the deal. Absolutely not, he'd make a fool of himself. The fans would be able to see through it in a heartbeat, and besides….

"Nobody said I'd have to kiss him." His words came out all hissed and hoarse. Kissing was *not* part of the original plan. He sure as hell would've noticed, and he was pretty sure he wouldn't have signed off on it.

Tara gave him a guilty look, but Abby bustled into the room at just that moment. Her hair was sleek and dark as usual. She looked efficient and a little pissed off.

"Did you tell Romeo and Romeo what the next move is?"

"Kiss at…."

"The *Cloud City* premiere. It's next Friday. We want classy, we want sweet, we want a fairy-tale kiss. Is that good?"

"Define good," Kerry said. He knew his face was sour. But he didn't like when people pulled shit on him, and this was the exact definition of pulling shit. What was next, the heated make-out session outside of a nightclub? Groping on the beach? Kerry wondered if this was the time to remind them that he was not, in fact, actually an actor, and he was most certainly not interested in kissing Jericho Knox.

"It's not a big deal," Jericho said from the corner. "You don't have to freak out about it. Just a stage kiss, man."

"I…." How did Kerry tell this room full of glamorous people that he'd only kissed three people in his whole life and two of them were long-term boyfriends and one of them was a boy behind the gym in middle school who usually pretended Kerry didn't exist? That the tiny bit of experience he had would never be enough to pull off a convincing long-term relationship kiss with a guy he barely knew and pretty much couldn't stand.

He didn't, that's how.

"Okay. Kiss at the movie premiere."

"Yes, and there will be a few after-parties that will be heaven for society photographers. You two will be at a couple of those, looking adorable together as well," Tara said. "I'll be with you for at least one of them. You'll have fun."

"Fun." Kerry somehow doubted it.

Chapter Seven

KERRY remembered back when he'd been in school, dreaming of the glamour of his future job—movie premieres, cocktails, trips to Cannes, expensive tuxedos. He'd always been smiling in those dreams, laughing at some faceless but fabulous celebrity's witty jokes. He'd been *happy*.

Somehow, things had turned out exactly the opposite of all of those dreams.

He woke up most days dreading what he'd have to do. Sometimes it wasn't much, just go to work and make sure someone—a fan, a pap, a passerby—saw him leaving Jericho's house in Jericho's flashy spare sports car; he'd definitely been lying about only driving a motorcycle. That much was clear when Kerry got a gander at his garage.

Sometimes it was a little worse. He'd need to post an Instagram picture, something cute and cuddly that Jericho inevitably didn't want to participate in. Kerry would get to listen to his griping and bitching until he finally capitulated and did what neither of them wanted to do. Kerry realized that their company worked for Jericho, but sometimes it was hard not to gripe right back, remind him that it wasn't Kerry who'd gotten his board waxed in a nightclub bathroom and caused a huge scandal.

One thing he didn't expect was… this. He was in his room at Jericho's house, with Tara and Abby hovering nearby examining him, acting as stylists. They'd brought over a suit earlier, one that had been painstakingly tailored to play up every one of his best assets and probably cost more than a couple months of his rent. The suit was dark charcoal gray with tiny flecks of an almost shimmery pale gray and the shirt underneath was a vibrant fuchsia that they'd chosen because of how it would show off his pale skin and dark hair.

"You look gorgeous, babe," Tara said. "Everyone's going to drool."

"What's Jericho wearing?" he asked.

"Black and white with a pocket square to match your shirt."

"Seriously?"

Tara grinned. "Yes. We want to present a cohesive team with you two. It'll be romantic."

"You don't think it's corny?" Kerry thought it was corny.

"No. You two will be perfect together."

Kerry wasn't so sure about that. They were pretty much toxic together, no matter what the public seemed to see in carefully set up pictures. They could pull it off one snap at a time, but how the hell were they going to act like a loving, comfortable, engaged couple live, on video, for the entire length of the red carpet?

"You ready?" Jericho asked from the door.

Kerry nearly swallowed his tongue. Jericho always looked hot, annoyingly so, but with a suit and his hair pulled back so perfectly, he looked like a god. Kerry hated that he was so attracted to him. At least in his moments of weakness.

"I'm ready."

As ready as I'm going to be.

A car was waiting for them at Jericho's door. The paps had eased over the past week or two. Kerry was actually wondering if he could go home and finish the remainder of this ridiculous stunt from the comfort of his own tiny room. He was getting tired of how it felt to be unwanted. Kerry slid into the car and as far into the corner as he could. He put his seatbelt on and smoothed his trousers so they wouldn't wrinkle.

As soon as Jericho got in the car, they pulled away. Kerry kept his eyes out the window, didn't even attempt to look at Jericho. He was so tired of bickering, tired of feeling guilty for helping the guy, like he was trying to get his foot in the door of celebdom. Kerry damn well knew he wasn't, but somehow Jericho had even managed to convince him he wanted something more out of this than to keep his own job. It was insane. So it was easier for him not to talk.

He watched the trees stream by as they drove down the hill toward the highway that would take them into the city. He wished he could be more excited about the night. It was his *first* movie premiere, after all. He only felt nervous. And worried. Kerry bit at his lips. The closer they got to the theater, the red carpet, the fans, and the hundreds of cameras, the more worried he got.

"Hey."

Kerry was surprised Jericho had spoken to him. Usually he chose not to say anything until somebody was watching. Kerry didn't even answer at first. He kind of figured they'd said all they needed to say to each other.

"Kerry. What's up?"

"Wow, you know my name." Kerry couldn't help it. He rolled his eyes and looked out the window.

"You don't need to be an asshole," Jericho said.

"Never stopped you before, did it?"

Jericho was silent for a long time, and Kerry wondered if he'd gone too far. Jericho was the client, after all. Then he let out a quiet breath. "Fair enough."

"Yeah." Kerry couldn't think of anything better to say.

"Are you okay?" Jericho asked. "You seem freaked out. More than usual."

Kerry let out a sarcastic little laugh. "How exactly am I supposed to be okay?" he asked.

"Is it the kiss?"

"*Yes*, it's the kiss." Kerry felt like letting out a frustrated scream. "We've barely said twenty sentences to each other in private, and I'm supposed to kiss you and make it look like I mean it? Like we've been together long enough that I've kissed you a thousand times?"

Jericho scooted closer. "Kerry. You can do this."

Kerry shook his head. "You want to know how many people I've kissed in my whole damn life? Three. Yeah, three. Two boyfriends and one boy who decided afterward that he was definitely straight. We were twelve."

"You've… only kissed three people?" Jericho looked taken aback. Pitying. Fantastic.

"Yes. And now I have to kiss you, and no offense, but it's not exactly going to be an easy task faking that kind of intimacy. I mean the last time I—"

Jericho lunged forward and kissed him.

Kissed him like he *meant* it. It wasn't hard, or brushing and tentative; it was a warm, familiar kiss, deep with a little bit of tongue and Jericho's hand in his hair. They kept kissing for several long, quiet seconds. Kerry's heart beat like one of those clichéd drums he always heard about. He got a melting shiver up his spine, and he actually wanted to lean closer. To Jericho.

Then Jericho pulled back gently, and they sat there breathing hard and staring at each other for a good thirty seconds. Jericho wiped a gentle thumb down Kerry's cheekbone.

"I think you'll be fine out there," Jericho said. "Just follow my lead like right now, and everything will go perfectly."

He kissed me….

Kerry was stunned, like, he could picture those tiny little cartoon birds swirling around his head kind of stunned. Jericho had kissed him. And it had been kind of amazing.

Kerry could nearly feel the crowd through the floor of the car as they pulled up. The noise pulsed against the doors and made the windows vibrate. Jericho reached over and put a hand on his knee.

"Listen, I know I'm not the easiest person to work with," Jericho said. Kerry giggled, partly out of nerves and partly from the vast understatement. "But thank you. I'm actually kind of glad it's you doing this instead of someone else."

"Why?" Kerry had been fairly sure Jericho hated him. What could be worse?

"You're cute. And I actually think if we'd met somewhere else, in a different situation, I might like to kiss you for real."

"Oh...." How the hell was he supposed to respond to that?

"Ready?" Jericho asked.

"Y-yeah." *No.*

"Then let's go."

Jericho waited for the driver to open his door, and he stepped out. Then he held his hand to Kerry and gave him a wink.

"It's showtime," he whispered.

Kerry gathered his mental strength and then gave Jericho his hand.

IT took about fifteen minutes for Kerry to feel like he could breathe again after they were done with the cacophony of the red carpet. The kiss, well that hadn't been a huge problem after their little warm-up in the car. Jericho had actually been a master—he'd pulled Kerry in right after he finished explaining to a journalist how they'd met, or at least a fictional version of it. The kiss had been natural, sweet, and actually more intimate than some of Kerry's real kisses. Just like every other time he'd gone out with Jericho and was treated to the looks, the cuddles and the handholding, it had started to feel real. Well, at least it had until they got into the premiere.

Jericho flashed a quick look at Kerry, dismissive in a way, and then melted into the crowd without a single word about it. Kerry was left standing in the lobby of the theater with a ton of people around him and zero armor. He'd never felt so naked. He'd been having a lot of those moments lately, like the whole world was watching him make a damn fool of himself, but it was worse when he hadn't been expecting it. When Jericho's colleagues peered curiously at him, he knew what they were thinking. Kerry swallowed around the thick lump in his throat.

Someone jostled him and tears welled up. It was dramatic, sure, but he felt like such an ass standing there all on his own. He decided to find the bar and stay there. Preferably with a large, strong drink. Kerry didn't know what else he was supposed to do.

Tara was there somewhere, and she'd promised to come save him as soon as she could, but she was working, and until she was done, he was stuck. If he went into the theater area and sat in their seats, he'd look like a huge loser. He couldn't mingle as Kerry the PR person, because, well, nobody was supposed to know him as that, so he was Kerry, Jericho's fiancé, who'd taken a near-permanent seat by the bar. He figured he'd better use it.

One screwdriver turned into two and then three. He'd been sitting there by himself for nearly an hour, and he was starting to feel a little drunk. And fragile. Where the hell was Tara? Jericho, well, Kerry hadn't seen his face since they walked in the door, and he supposed he didn't expect to. He was so out of his league.

Out of nowhere, Jericho came floating from the crowd. He looked a bit tipsy, but he was smiling at Kerry like they were actually friends. "What are you doing back here?" he asked. "I was supposed to introduce you around, remember?" Jericho gave him a significant look.

"I don't know. I'm not the one who decided to play Where's Waldo the second we got in here. I was just waiting."

"Well, come. Meet some people. And smile. My new director is here, and I don't want to give him a bad impression."

"Yeah. Would hate that."

"*Kerry.*"

"I'll be fine. I'll do my job."

KERRY didn't think there would be anything he hated more than swimming through a sea of paparazzi. He was so, so wrong. Getting dragged around a premiere like Jericho Knox's new puppy had to have been the worst night of his life. It wasn't Jericho, actually, for the first time probably ever. Jericho played his part to perfection—all the glances and chuckles and touches, even a few fond forehead kisses looked and felt real. It was everyone else, at least most of them.

He'd never felt so judged in his entire life.

It was like their disdain for the guy from *the picture* seeped out of their pores and drilled into him. They were polite on the surface, at least, but their smiles were less than genuine, and they looked at him like some sideshow act in a perverted carnival when Jericho glanced away. *There's the guy who sucked Jericho off in public*, their eyes said. *Doesn't he have any shame?* their pursed lips asked. Jericho didn't get the same judgment. Either it was because they knew him, because he wasn't the one performing the act, or just because he was a celeb and Kerry wasn't, he somehow escaped judgment. Kerry wanted to tell them all it wasn't him; it wasn't *him* in the picture, so quit fucking looking at him like he had the plague. Obviously that was out of the question.

He was almost grateful when Jericho planted him back at the bar. "Let me talk to my director for a minute. Then I'll come back, and we can get to our seats," Jericho said. He gave Kerry a friendly smile, a real smile, and even a kiss on the forehead, and then he was off before Kerry even had a chance to answer.

"See you in a few," he murmured to himself. Kerry ordered another drink, a gin and tonic instead of a screwdriver for a change. He was relieved to be away from the whole pony show, but he hated sitting alone. He hadn't seen Tara other than a wave from across the room. Kerry was so beyond wanting to leave. He wondered if anyone would notice. He stayed at the bar for close to another half an hour before someone took the seat next to him.

"He's not going to stay with you, you know."

"What?" Kerry thought maybe the woman wasn't talking to him.

"Jericho Knox. He's not meant to be tied down. Plus, this whole bisexual thing has to be a phase. He's too much of a pussy hound for it to last."

Kerry was too stunned to answer at first. The woman shrugged and pulled a lipgloss from her bag. She took her time putting it on and then tossed it back into her bag and clipped it shut. Kerry still stared.

"Why would you say that to me?" he asked.

"Just passing out some truth. Get whatever it is you're looking for—a YouTube following, your own part on some two-bit werewolf show. Soon enough

Jericho will get tired of you, and everyone in this room, and everywhere else, will start to say what they really think of the little whore who has a picture of himself sucking dick splashed all over the Internet."

Kerry felt like he was going to be sick. Sure, she just said what everyone had to be thinking, and it wasn't news to him, but to *hear* it like that? Maybe it was the way she said it, so raunchy and to the point; maybe it was that he'd seen her words in every single person's eyes. Maybe it was that he'd had four drinks on an empty stomach and Kerry was a lightweight on his best day.

He toppled off his stool and went for an exit; he had to get out of there immediately. Kerry couldn't sit through a whole movie that he didn't even care about, thinking about what she'd said, thinking about the way everyone looked at him, what they must be thinking still. He had to go home. Like *home* home. He found a side exit and slipped out the door.

It was hot outside, not the refreshing change he'd been hoping for, and the alley smelled a bit off, like garbage and maybe something worse, but he was free. Kerry started walking away from the main street in front of the theater and away from the craphole his life had turned into. He pulled out his phone from his slacks and called the one person he knew would come for him anytime he needed him.

Cole picked up right away. "What's up, Ker. I thought you were in a movie?"

"Can you come get me?" Kerry knew his voice sounded thick. "I don't have a car, and I don't want one of Jericho's fans to see me get in a cab. I need to get out of here."

"Yeah. Text me an address. I'm getting my keys right now."

Kerry found a corner and texted Cole his address. It was a long wait, most of which Kerry spent cursing horrible Los Angeles traffic. Finally, though, the telltale rumble of Cole's beat-up Bronco came around the corner, a sound Kerry had never been so happy to hear. He checked to make sure they were reasonably alone and then jogged to the Bronco and got in.

"Hey. Thanks for coming to get me."

"No problem. Where are we going?"

"Home. Let's go home."

IT took Jericho about twenty minutes of looking before he realized there was no way Kerry was still at the premiere. He pulled out his phone to text him, but he didn't even have Kerry's damn number.

Jericho wanted to scream, but he smiled at the people he passed on his way out to the alley. He pressed dial on the number he did in fact have. Tara picked up after three rings.

"Jericho?" she asked. "Aren't you supposed to be at the premiere? I just saw you a few minutes ago. Please tell me you didn't leave. Why are you calling me?"

"That would be a good question to ask your boy, who took off without even telling me he was leaving. I need his phone number. Can you text it to me?"

"Kerry just left?" Tara sounded as shocked as Jericho felt. He'd never had someone who didn't cooperate just because… well, probably Kerry didn't cooperate because Jericho had ditched him. And he had; he knew it. It had felt pretty damn good to get away there for a few minutes. Jericho looked at his watch. Or nearly two hours. Shit. Stunt or not, annoyed or not, that wasn't the person his parents had raised him to be.

"Yeah. I think I left him to fend for himself a bit too long among the sharks."

"You left him alone? On his first major outing with industry people who have to be looking down their noses at him after the story broke? Jericho, how could you?"

"He shouldn't have left the damn event." Jericho tried to keep his voice down, but it was hard. He wasn't happy, and he'd never been the calm, quiet type when he was angry.

"I'll text you his number. You know… you seem pretty angry at Kerry," Tara said. "It's not exactly fair, and I don't get where the animosity is coming from."

It was probably the most serious Tara had ever sounded. Jericho shrugged even though she couldn't see him.

"I guess I don't know what his agenda is. It makes me worry about what he's getting out of this and how it could blow back on me."

"What the hell, Jericho. Agenda? Kerry's only agenda is to get through this, not get fired for being uncooperative, and move on with his life."

"What?" Jericho wondered what part of the story he'd missed. "Who said anything about firing him if he didn't do it?"

He thought he remembered Kerry bringing it up once or twice, but to be honest, Jericho had a habit of not hearing what he didn't want to hear. He cringed.

"Nobody. But it was implied quite heavily. I think you would've picked it up if you weren't too busy being pissed off at the world and the mess that you created all by yourself. The mess Kerry's trying to get you out of."

"Tough love, Tara." He was too puzzled by her uncharacteristic outburst to be annoyed by the way she'd talked to him.

"You need it. Now get off the phone and go find Kerry."

Jericho hung up and waited for the buzz to come with Kerry's phone number. He dialed the number when he got it and waited for Kerry to pick up. Which he didn't. Jericho decided to text.

Kerry. Where are you? I'll come pick you up. This is Jericho.

He didn't get an answer for a few long minutes. Jericho called for the car and wished like hell he'd brought one of his own.

I'm home.

My place?

No. Home.

Can I have an address? I'll come get you.

The phone buzzed again with an address. Jericho gave the address to the driver as soon as he slid into the backseat, and spent the drive to Kerry's place in silence. He felt kind of bad, to be honest. He wasn't really all that good at apologizing, though. And he was still pissed at Kerry for leaving the premiere. It was his job to stay. And Jericho had kind of liked knowing he was there waiting in the background. Whatever sense that made.

Kerry's apartment building wasn't anything special. Kind of crappy. Jericho was less than impressed. He texted Kerry again and asked if he wanted him to come up or if he was going to come down. Kerry said he'd be down in a minute. Jericho didn't know if it was possible to read tone from a text, but he sure as hell didn't seem enthused to be hearing from Jericho. Or getting in a car with him.

When he came down, he wasn't wearing the gorgeous tailored suit anymore, but instead an old pair of sweats that hung off his hips and round little butt, and a thin T-shirt. He had on flip-flops and glasses, and Jericho wanted to eat him. He remembered kissing him earlier, the sweet shock, and the way Kerry melted into his touch. He… wanted to do it again. No act necessary. Which wasn't exactly the best idea in the world.

"What?" Kerry said.

"You getting in the car?" He noticed Kerry had his wallet and keys, so he had to expect to go back with Jericho.

"Yeah. Fine." Kerry slid in. He didn't say anything else to Jericho, though, just looked out the window.

"I'm sorry I ditched you in there," Jericho said. "You didn't have to leave, you know. I was trying to find you."

"When you texted? I was already home by then."

"Why'd you leave?" Jericho asked. "You were supposed to stay. People will have noticed that I'm gone." He knew he sounded snappy. It wasn't easy for him to let go of his irritation, even if he'd been partly to blame.

"She called me a whore, Jericho. She said you'd get tired of me and go back to women, which is fine. I don't really care about that, but she called me a *whore*. I couldn't stay there anymore."

Jericho didn't know what made him do it, but he reached out and pulled Kerry into a hug.

"I'm sorry," he whispered. "I think I've really misjudged you, and no matter what, you didn't deserve that."

"You think?" Kerry asked. He snorted, but it sounded more like he was trying to get rid of tears than show actual sarcasm.

"Yeah. I think." Jericho felt a hard, guilty pit in his stomach. He thought he was savvier than that, better at judging people and dealing with them accordingly. How could he have screwed up so bad?

"Great." Kerry scrunched down in the seat and made himself look tiny. Something painful twisted in Jericho's chest. *Fuck, I'm an asshole.*

"Listen, can we start over?"

"I don't know, depends on what starting over means. I certainly don't want a repeat of the past two weeks. They've pretty much sucked."

"I deserved that. Shit." Jericho ground his thumbs into his eyes and massaged away a growing headache. "We still have a lot of time ahead of us. I just think it would be better if we were friends and not this—" Kerry went to speak, but Jericho held up his hand. "I know it's my fault that we're like this. I know. So that's why I asked. Can we start over?"

Kerry seemed to think about it for a few seconds, then sighed. "I don't have the energy to be a bitch to you, so I guess so. It's really not who I am, even if I do hate what you assumed about me."

"I don't assume it anymore. You're just trying to do your job."

"Preaching to the choir over here." Kerry rolled his eyes. "I've been trying to tell you all along."

"So… friends?"

Kerry smiled tentatively. "We'll work on it."

Chapter Eight

KERRY thought it would get easier over time. It had been nearly a month, after all—a month of dates and picture ops, events and him sneaking in and out of his office building by the back door so nobody would see where he worked. He had practice and lots of it. But it hadn't gotten any easier.

He still was taken aback when he went out for lunch with Tara and some fan of Jericho's asked for a picture with him. He was surprised when they talked about him on Twitter. Some part of him expected the huge burst at the beginning, and then he thought it would fade, but it *hadn't*. He'd gotten his own fans, as odd and misguided as it was, and they seemed to like him as much as they liked Jericho. They barely knew anything about him, and they liked him. Or hated him, because some of

Jericho's groupies weren't exactly fans of him taking their future boyfriend or husband away. Even though he'd come to the realization over the past few years that the entertainment business was far less glamour than he'd originally thought, experiencing it from this side was kind of the final straw or something. It wasn't real. Nothing was real. And Kerry hated it.

He'd been planning to stop off and hang out at home with Cole and Robbie after work, but there was someone following him. He noticed a few miles away from work that the same car was behind him. It looked like a few girls, and they definitely had their phones filming him.

Jesus.

He wasn't going home, after all. Instead of going toward his apartment he turned toward Topanga and Jericho's house. He really had wanted a break from Jericho and the house and the whole thing. He'd wanted to watch a damn movie with his brother and roommate and just not be Kerry the Notorious for one damn night. Not likely. Maybe he could invite Cole and Robbie over to Jericho's. George had encouraged him to make it look like Jericho was close with his family. He seriously just needed a break and some people he actually loved.

There were only a few paps camped at Jericho's gate—they had to be a setup, because there was no way he and Jericho were still genuinely that big of news. Kerry wondered why until he saw Jericho pulling up the hill on his motorcycle.

Oh.

Tara or Abby must've set up a photo op. He wished they'd have passed it by him like they had with most of the details so he was at least aware of the schedule.

Jericho noticed him and blew him a kiss, Kerry opened the gate for him since he had a remote handy, and Jericho started to drive through. A few of the paps must've decided to try to get a reaction out of them.

"You must like not having to work anymore."

"How's it feel to be a gold digger?"

"I'd probably suck his cock in public for a house like this too."

Kerry didn't know what to do. Usually—with the exception of the dick at the yogurt shop—the guys they hired to come get fluff pictures were polite; maybe they asked a few questions but were generally unobtrusive as long as they got their shots.

"Hey, asshole. That's why I kept this private for so long. I don't want you guys hassling him."

Jericho looked genuinely angry. He hopped off his bike and came down the drive to where Kerry was trying to get in without hitting any of them. They wouldn't let him pass.

"Get out of his way. Leave my fiancé alone."

The few paps hanging out snapped picture after picture of Jericho's angry face and his gesturing arms.

"Babe, just push on the gas. They'll move eventually."

"I don't want to hit them," Kerry said. That was the last thing any of them needed.

"They'll move. Just drive slowly." Jericho ran around and got into the passenger seat of the car. Kerry started moving, and eventually the two stubborn ones got out of his way. They closed the gate behind them.

"Shit," Kerry whispered once he'd finally gotten to the garage and shut off the car.

"You okay?"

"No. Today sucked. I had the longest day ever, and I just wanted to see my brother, but these fans were following me, so I came here, and then there were those paps, and—" Kerry slapped the steering wheel. "Ouch!"

"Hey." Jericho reached over and cupped his face.

"You don't have to do that. Nobody can see us."

"I know." Jericho pulled him across the gearshift into an awkward but comforting side hug. "Do you want to bring your brother over here? I know what it's like when you first get dragged into this world. You've got to be overwhelmed."

"Why are you being so nice?"

Jericho hadn't been *awful* the past couple of days, but they hadn't decided to be besties either, just a lot more cordial.

"I actually kind of like you, despite my best efforts originally, and I'm not a complete asshole."

Kerry gave him a long look.

"Okay, mostly I am, but I'm trying not to be. But do you want to bring your brother over or not?"

"Can our other roommate come too? He knows what's going on."

"I thought the rule was family only."

"Robbie is family. Plus, if I didn't tell him the truth, he'd have been here slamming on your door so he could kick your ass. He's already hinted that he'd enjoy doing that as it is." White lie. Kerry might have enjoyed watching Jericho squirm.

"And you want this guy in my pool?"

"He'll behave."

COLE and Robbie showed up less than an hour later with a stack of pizzas and a few sixers of craft beer.

"Holy fuck" was the first thing out of Robbie's mouth.

"He's not housebroken yet. I apologize." Kerry winced.

"Sorry, dude, I've never been anywhere this nice before."

"Um, come in," Jericho said. "Hi. I'm Jericho."

"No kidding." Cole still wasn't impressed with Jericho. He'd made that very clear to Kerry on a number of occasions.

"Cole, knock it off." Kerry elbowed him. He didn't want his brother to make things even more awkward. Kerry was *not* interested in going back to where they were before the night of the premiere. There was still way too much summer left to live like that.

"Sorry. Thanks for having us over. You have a great place." Cole gave Jericho the winning smile that usually made everyone love him. Jericho smiled back, hesitantly.

"You guys want to come in and eat before the pizza gets cold?" Kerry asked. He wanted to defuse the tension as much as possible. No use getting to spend time with his brother if it was going to be awkward all night.

"Yeah. Let's go out to the deck. It's a nice night, and, you know, who wants to be inside?" Jericho's smile was sweeter and less confident than anything Kerry had ever seen from him.

"Great." Kerry led Cole and Robbie out to the pool area. He hadn't spent a ton of time out there so far. It seemed to be Jericho's place to go when he wanted to be alone, and Kerry hadn't been very interested in interrupting that personal time and getting another nasty Jericho dress-down.

The pool deck was incredible, especially in the setting sun. Jericho's view was out of some sort of fantasy. The house was perched on the edge of the hills, and his pool and yard had a nearly three sixty view—the faded green of Topanga Canyon, the crescent of blue ocean beyond, flickering lights of the nighttime city waking up after a long day.

"Jesus," Cole muttered. "You've been living here all these weeks?"

"Yeah. Kind of." Kerry shrugged.

Cole smiled quietly at him like he knew what he meant. Jericho must've caught that, because he winced like he felt bad about it. It was true, though. Kerry might have been living at the house, but he spent most of his time in his bedroom. He cooked, sure, but he didn't hang out in the downstairs media room and play video games with Jericho. He didn't spend hours out by the pool taking in the insane view and barbecuing. On the surface, it seemed like a dream. In reality, it had been rather lacking.

They all settled in the cushy chairs that surrounded a rattan-and-glass outdoor coffee table.

"Can I put the pizzas on this table?" Robbie asked. Kerry didn't blame him. It looked more expensive than their entire apartment.

"Course. I'll go in and grab some plates and napkins. Do any of you guys want silverware or glasses?"

Robbie just stared at him. Kerry imagined he hadn't quite gotten over where they were. "Nah, I think we're good," Kerry said. Figured he'd save everyone from any more awkwardness.

Cole and Robbie broke into their typical brand of laughter and speed talking as soon as Jericho was gone.

"Holy shit, bro, this place is off the hook," Robbie crowed. "I'd be in the pool like twenty-four seven."

"I haven't been in it at all," Kerry said with a sad smile. "I'll have to make up for it tonight."

"You okay?" Cole asked. He'd always had a sixth sense for when Kerry was upset. It was kind of amazing how easily his brother read him.

"Yeah. I'm getting used to it, you know? It's crazy, like, who would've ever thought that I'd be used to paparazzi?"

"I hate that they take pictures of you like that."

Kerry shrugged. "It's part of the gig. Plus, it's not all the time, mostly just when we're places they expect us to be... or if George called them in for a photo shoot." He rolled his eyes. "You'd be shocked by how many of the celeb pap shots are planned."

"What, you mean all those pop stars and actresses don't come out of the gym in full makeup and dresses all the time?" Robbie asked. He and Cole snickered.

"No, of course that's completely natural and not set up." Kerry laughed along with them.

Jericho returned then with his fancy plates, a pile of napkins, and a smile. They all dug into the pizza, which happened to be Kerry's favorite. There was a stereotype that LA pizza sucked. Kerry had eaten pizza in New York once or twice. He called bullshit.

Dinner was actually a lot more relaxed than he'd anticipated. Jericho managed to charm a hesitant Cole and a starstruck Robbie a lot faster than Kerry expected. Soon they were all laughing and sipping on their beers.

"You guys want to hit the pool?" Jericho asked. "It's too nice of a night to waste the opportunity."

"Hell, yeah. I mean that sounds great," Robbie said.

Kerry grinned at him. "Follow me, guys. I'll show you where to change."

He led the guys through the high-ceilinged living room, giving them a cursory tour as they went. He showed them to the guest bathroom off the hallway.

"Here, if you two want to take turns or whatever, I'll be right out." Kerry pointed. "My room is down the hall here."

"Where's Jericho's?" Cole asked.

"Upstairs. I actually haven't even seen up there."

Cole made a face. "Good."

"I thought you were starting to like him. You seemed to have a good time at dinner," Kerry said.

"Yeah, but liking him in general and thinking he's good enough for you are two different things. I was afraid the lines were going to blur."

Kerry decided it was best not to tell his brother exactly how much the lines had blurred for him on occasion.

"Nah. Strictly professional. Don't worry."

"Mom and Dad still hate this, you know."

"Yeah. I know. Mom's made it pretty clear she wants me to quit and come home. She doesn't like what LA has done to me, she says."

"As long as you're okay," Cole said.

"Yeah. I'm okay."

Sort of. Kerry hadn't really grasped just how hard it would be until he was living it. How hard it would be sometimes to tell the difference between reality and an act, how much he hated seeing his face in the tabloids, how much he missed being a nobody with a nobody job who went home to his comfortable nobody apartment. He wondered how quickly he'd be forgotten after this. When he'd be able to slip into his old life and be that person again. He wondered if it would be weird when he got there, or if it would feel like it always had. Whatever. Not much he could do about it anyway.

"See you in a few, Bro." He clapped Cole on the shoulder.

"I'VE been waiting for you to touch me." Kerry giggled and looked up at Jericho from the sheets. They were bright white against his dark shock of hair. Jericho reached down and ran his finger through Kerry's hair. It felt like heated silk. He cupped Kerry's cheek and leaned over for a long, deep kiss.

Kerry's lips tasted like they had the last time, like peaches and mint gum and everything Jericho wanted to kiss again and again. But even better was his skin. It was soft, pale, and it made Jericho want to sink in.

"Touch me," Kerry murmured. He rolled his hips under Jericho and dragged a hand down Jericho's chest. It was the hottest thing Jericho had ever seen. He couldn't decide what to do first—he wanted to taste and touch and sink into Kerry's warm body. He wanted it all. Kerry wrapped his legs around Jericho's hips and—

HIS phone alarm buzzed, insistent and seriously annoying. Jericho groaned and hauled himself out of bed. He didn't even need to be up, he'd just forgotten to turn off the alarm on his phone the night before, which pissed him off. He was awake, though, and turned on, so he hopped into a quick shower to rinse off and deal with some things. He felt a little guilty. After all, Kerry was trying to be professional and friendly, and Kerry would never know what Jericho had just dreamed about. He couldn't. Jericho dressed in a T-shirt and a low-hanging pair of Adidas pants and wandered downstairs.

"Kerry?" he called quietly.

Kerry wasn't going in to the office that day, but he was usually up far before Jericho, even on days he didn't have to be. Jericho was greeted by silence. Then he looked down the hall and noticed Kerry's bedroom door hanging open. He walked down and looked in. Kerry's bed was neatly made and his jacket hung on one of the hooks on the wall. His laptop bag was on the chair near the closet, as were the shoes he usually wore to work. His running shoes were nowhere to be seen, though. Jericho figured that's where he'd gone.

And then he realized that he knew what shoes Kerry had with him and what his patterns were. A flash of the dream, of creamy skin and breathy moans, flashed into Jericho's head.

Shit.

He rushed down the hall and away from Kerry's room before he was caught looking in there—by whom, Jericho didn't know. But nobody ever said impulses were rational.

By the time Jericho finished his coffee, Kerry was wandering in the front door. He had on shorts and a tank top, he was sweaty, and he looked delectable. Too delectable. Jericho was suddenly very uncomfortably aware of his dream and how much he liked kissing Kerry, even if it was just for show, or how much he'd like to kiss him for no reason other than the fact that it would feel good.

No. You don't think about him like that. Stop.

"What were you doing?" Jericho snapped. He nearly cringed when he realized he'd been pissy because he wanted to kiss Kerry, and he felt guilty as hell about it.

"What's your problem?" Kerry asked. He pushed around Jericho and started for his bedroom.

"My problem is the paps. What if they'd swarmed you out there? You know George has them on us constantly right now."

"Jericho. You're freaking out over nothing. There weren't even any paps out there today."

"Just because you didn't see them doesn't mean they weren't there."

"So the… invisible paps who I can't see are going to attack me out of nowhere because I'm out running, me, the nonfamous half of this equation?"

Jericho felt kind of stupid when Kerry put it that way. "Okay."

Kerry burst out laughing. "What the hell was that all about? I forgot for a moment I wasn't with my mom."

"Did you just call me your mom?"

"Did you just warn me about invisible nonpaps?"

They both stared at each other for a long moment. Jericho couldn't help laughing. He dissolved into very unmanly giggles.

"Seriously," Kerry said when he caught his breath. "What are you *on*?"

Jericho tried to figure out what to tell him. *I freaked out because I had a sex dream about you* wasn't it.

"I, uh, had a nightmare. I guess I hadn't shaken it off yet."

"I'd hate to see you after a scary movie," Kerry said.

"I'm sorry for flipping out on you."

Kerry paused and stared. "Did I just get an apology from the great Jericho Knox?"

"Yeah. I guess so."

"That's two in a week." He made a mock fainting gesture. "Miracles are real."

Jericho pushed him. "Shut up."

THE rest of the day was relaxing to a point, or it would have been if Jericho didn't keep picturing Kerry naked and writhing underneath him. They did some work from the side of the pool—or rather Kerry did. Jericho didn't have much to do, so he read a few magazines and swam some laps.

In the afternoon, Kerry went to grab a late lunch with his brother, so Jericho called his mom. They talked a lot more often than most people would probably believe, given his reputation. They probably also wouldn't believe she was one of his best friends. He hadn't called her much lately, and had avoided a number of her calls to him. It was mostly because he couldn't bear to talk to her about the picture and the fallout that had come from it, but he'd missed hearing her voice.

"Jericho, darling," she said before he even had a chance to greet her. "I've been worried about you with all those stories in the paper."

He'd been intensely embarrassed that his mother had seen the picture in the club. Unlike Kerry, he couldn't tell the people close to him that it wasn't him in the picture, because it was. He also wasn't going to try to convince Caroline Knox that he and Kerry were for real—she was a lot smarter than that, and she knew he would've told her about Kerry the moment it happened. So she was on board with the image cleanup, and after Jericho explained to her that Kerry was just trying to do his job and wanted nothing as far as fame went, she was on board with him as well.

"I'm actually a lot better than I thought I'd be," he told her.

"Good. Are you taking care of yourself?" she asked.

"Yeah, Ma. I'm good. I'm eating well, exercising, I haven't been drinking much."

"Good," she said again. Emphatically.

"I'm sorry you have to go through all this. Are people giving you a hard time at home?"

His mom didn't answer, which meant yes, they were. Jericho decided he needed to pay a little visit to his neighborhood and see what he could do.

"I don't think I'll ever understand your job. Why do you want people to see your private life like this?" she said.

"Sometimes it doesn't seem worth it, but then sometimes it seems like this was all I was meant to do and if I can't be an actor, then I don't know what I'll do with my life."

"Can't you be an actor without all of this?"

"Hopefully soon. I'm not at that place in my career yet where my work is all I need. Maybe this show will be what gets me there."

"I really hope so, darling. I hate this for you. Don't worry about me. I'm tough."

Jericho laughed. His mom had made that fact very clear over the years. She was as tough as they came.

"Hey, I'd better go. My trainer is going to be here in a little bit. Can you give Dad a hug for me and tell him I say sorry to him too."

"Don't worry about your father, sweetie. Just get through this."

"I am. I love you, Ma."

"I love you too."

Jericho hung up the phone and realized he didn't spend nearly enough time being grateful for his family. They put up with a lot of crap because of him. He jogged up the stairs to his room to change before his trainer got there. Jericho really liked Rich, and he hated to make him wait.

By the time Kerry got home, Jericho had worked out, showered, and was hanging out in the shade near the pool with a book he'd been meaning to read for months. Since it wasn't a good idea for him to be seen out alone anymore, at least not in any of his usual haunts, Jericho had been flying through his reading list. He had to admit, after a few days of restlessness, it was kind of… nice.

"What do you want for dinner?" Kerry asked.

Jericho chuckled. "Didn't you just eat lunch?"

"Like three hours ago. Cole and I walked down Venice for a while."

"Did you get your picture taken?"

"Yeah, but Abby made sure to let all the photo agencies know Cole was my brother so they could label the pictures the right way. Don't want to be accidentally cheating on you with him in the morning tabloids." Kerry made a face.

Jericho giggled. "My mom was my cougar girlfriend a few times before they got it right. I don't know what she was more offended by—the fact that they thought she was dating her son, or that they called her a cougar."

Kerry laughed out loud at that. Jericho loved his laugh—open, happy, beautiful. "Why don't I cook tonight?" Kerry asked. "I got some great salmon, the last of the Copper River, and we could have a salad and some ice cream."

"Not going to complain about any of that. I can do the salad if you want to make the salmon."

Jericho was struck about halfway through making dinner when he realized he'd been laughing and talking with Kerry and it felt like a *date*. A real one. Jericho didn't have much experience with real dates. He'd only been on a couple in his entire life. But when he hip-checked Kerry away from his sauce with a laugh, and Kerry winked at him, and Jericho wanted so desperately to lean over and kiss him because it just felt *right*, that's when he knew it wasn't an act. The heat in his belly wasn't an act. How much he loved Kerry's smell and his eyes and his laugh wasn't an act. Jericho put his spoon down on the stovetop and turned. Kerry was making his way to the fruit rack for a lemon, and Jericho couldn't help it. He reached out and pulled Kerry close.

"Okay?" Jericho asked.

Kerry got it. He knew. "Okay," Kerry said.

Jericho leaned over, like he'd wanted to do for *days*, and he kissed Kerry.

Chapter Nine

KERRY was exhausted. A hell of a lot happier than he'd been at the beginning of summer but exhausted. Who would've thought that a few photo ops and some events added to his work schedule would be enough to wear him out, but they were. At least things were good with him and Jericho. Very good, actually, but still confusing as hell. They'd *kissed*. More than once. A very large part of him still couldn't believe that was something that had happened in his life. He'd kissed Jericho Knox. He was living with Jericho Knox. Kerry was surprised how easy it was to separate moody, unpredictable, vulnerable Jericho from confident, charming, dangerous Jericho Knox. It was almost like they were two different people, twins with the same face but completely different personalities.

And they'd *kissed*.

Yeah, a few of those were public, or at the very least prepping for public, but some of the more recent ones... hadn't been. Some of them had been seeking and gentle and very much in private and not for anyone to see. Kerry still remembered how Jericho had crowded him up against the kitchen counter the night before, lifted him and slid his hands under Kerry's shirt. He remembered the gentle brush of his lips, the way they breathed like they were meant to breathe the same air. And the way he'd casually offered Kerry some tea afterward, like it was the most natural and nonconfusing thing to do after a kiss that wasn't supposed to happen according to every contract they'd signed. So kissing was a thing they did now. And he didn't know what to think about it. Jericho sure as hell wasn't saying anything. Kerry decided he wasn't going to either.

Pap pictures, events... and lots of kissing.

Whatever that meant.

HE was broken out of his moment of staring at the screen of his laptop when Jericho knocked on the door.

"Yeah?" Kerry asked. He still wasn't to the point where it was comfortable in Jericho's house. He felt like he was tiptoeing around a lot, never sure if he was going to get the charming actor, the moody overgrown boy, or the third option, which was very new—soft and oddly romantic. It was seriously unsettling.

"Can I come in?" Jericho asked.

"Of course."

The door cracked open, and Jericho poked in his head. "I was going to see if you wanted Thai for dinner.

I've been in the mood all week, and my favorite place delivers. At least they will for me."

"Personalized delivery service?" Kerry asked. He rolled his eyes, but it was hard not to smile.

"They put the policy in place the last time a bunch of fans figured out I was there and basically blockaded the entrance. I apologized forever and try to order from them as often as I can and tip outrageously."

Kerry had to grin, even though the little story highlighted how big of a pain Jericho's life had to be. "I can see why you do that, I guess. What do they have that's good?"

"Everything." Jericho practically moaned. "What do you usually like?"

"Eggplant, if they have it. And spring rolls. And if they have coconut sticky rice with mangoes." Kerry snorted. "Wow, I'm being a pig."

"Um, you haven't heard my order. I'm pretty sure they have an eggplant dish. Let me pull up the menu on my phone."

So he was getting option four—friendly and casual. Or maybe a variation on option three. Kerry wasn't sure he'd seen this Jericho yet. He had to admit, he really liked this Jericho. "If they don't have that, just order me something good."

"You're giving me the choice?" Jericho chuckled. "I thought you were a picky eater."

"Just… no shrimp. Okay?"

"Okay."

Jericho slid out of his room with a smile, and Kerry heard his footsteps wandering down the hallway.

"Okay, then…."

He spent the next twenty-five minutes trying to focus on the work he had to finish if he didn't want to get an Abby smackdown, but finally he gave up. Right when he shut his laptop with a loud sigh, he heard the buzzer for the front gate.

He hopped out of bed and jogged to the door of his room.

"Do you want me to go out and get it?" Kerry called.

"Nah. I have it."

Kerry heard the front door shut, and he made his way down the hallway toward the main living area. Jericho came in minutes later with a huge grin and three groaning bags of food.

"Jessica, the daughter, was driving tonight. She just told me she got taken off the waiting list for Stanford. She's going in the fall." He looked nearly as proud as if she were his own kid.

"That's great. Do you talk to her often?"

"Yeah." He looked a little embarrassed. "They probably get tired of me, but I order from them pretty often. I don't get a lot of people who don't… want something from me. It's refreshing that they seem to not care who I am."

Kerry slipped past him to the kitchen to grab some plates and utensils. He thought about how Jericho had assumed he was looking for a leg up at the beginning. He imagined it came with the territory, and it made him feel a little bad for not getting where Jericho was coming from.

"You're not getting forks, are you?" Jericho asked.

"Um, yeah?"

"Not a chance. Chopsticks, babe."

Babe?

"You don't want me eating with chopsticks unless you plan to be here all night."

"You'll learn. You're hungry right?"

Kerry rolled his eyes and grabbed a fork anyway. It was a weird combination, the sensation of being in a place that so clearly wasn't his own and the blatant lack of regard he gave Jericho most of the time.

Jericho laughed.

"It's good to see you listen to me."

"Always."

DINNER was a whole new level of *different*. He and Jericho laughed, they talked, they ate delicious Thai food, and for the first time practically since the beginning, Kerry was completely comfortable.

"You know, I like this," Jericho said.

"Yeah," Kerry agreed quietly. "It's good."

"No, I meant just us. Hanging out. We've been doing it more, and it's nice."

"Oh." Kerry looked up and smiled. He'd been trying to spear the last piece of his eggplant with chopsticks—figured he'd give them a try after all—but he was failing miserably. "I like it too. You're a lot of fun to be around when you forget you're supposed to be moody and difficult."

Jericho laughed out loud at that. "My momma would be so proud to hear you say that. Do you have a lot of work to do, or do you want to watch a movie tonight?"

Kerry hadn't been invited to the inner sanctum of entertainment yet, so he was a little shocked. "Really?" he asked.

"Yeah. Come on. We can rent whatever you want."

Kerry nodded. "Sure. I don't really feel like finishing my work anyway."

They cleaned up the dinner leftovers and trailed down the stairs to the lower level of the house that included a gym he had used once or twice and the entertainment room he'd never been in.

Jericho gestured at a huge cushy couch.

"The air-conditioner in here gets pretty intense. There are blankets in the basket."

A wicker chest doubled as a coffee table. Kerry opened it and pulled out a blanket for himself and one for Jericho as well. Then he leaned back while Jericho performed some sort of techno-mating ritual. Finally the system burst into life with a main screen in large brilliant color right in front of them.

"I didn't know they made TVs this big," Kerry murmured.

"Yeah, they do." Jericho smiled. "What do you want to watch?"

Kerry shrugged. "Pick something. I work so much I haven't seen any of it."

"You've got to stop that." Jericho made a face.

"I'll keep it in mind."

WORK came early the next morning, and with it another meeting with the team. The Jericho team, as Kerry had started thinking of it, even though they all dealt with multiple clients. Jericho had just taken over his life, for good or for ill. Or a little bit of both. He felt a bit hungover from the dinner and movie, even though he hadn't drunk a single thing. Jericho was confusing as hell, and getting more confusing by the day, by the hour even. Dinner had been friendly, full of banter and laughter. The start of the movie, some slasher zombie flick that was more gore than plot, had been the same.

But halfway through the movie, Jericho had slung his arm over the couch. Seriously. Then he'd gotten a bit closer and pulled Kerry in like that was expected.

"I like to cuddle," he'd murmured as the only explanation.

Jericho Knox liked to cuddle. News Kerry probably had never needed. By the end of the movie, which had only gotten marginally better, Kerry had laid his head on Jericho's shoulder, since it was a hell of a lot more comfortable than holding it up, even with Jericho pulling him closer, and Jericho's fingers had found their way into the sensitive hairs on the back of Kerry's neck, where he'd scratched contentedly.

"You want to watch another one?" Jericho had whispered.

Kerry remembered thinking that it was a bad idea, that another movie with Jericho would end somewhere he really shouldn't go. But he'd said, yes. Like a fool. And it had ended exactly where he thought it would—with them lying flat on the couch, Jericho on top of him, kissing again.

Jericho didn't take it much further, just a bit of touching and that one moment when he slung Kerry's leg over his hip and ground down, which was… *hell*. Hot. But they'd kissed for a long, long time. Probably the longest Kerry had ever spent just kissing in his life. And Jericho was by far the best kisser he'd ever had. By far, like no comparison far.

So it was pretty understandable that he felt like a zombie when he got into the office the next morning. And even more understandable when he wanted to cry at the sticky note on his screen to meet for a meeting as soon as he got there.

"We're going to send you two on vacation," George announced. "A few days somewhere tropical, and then I want you to go meet his parents. In Charleston. Can you set up some local photographers and pick a pretty resort? I can get Tara to handle the rest as long as the framework is settled."

Kerry didn't even get to the locations. He was stuck on the fact that George wanted him to go spend time with Jericho's family. In their house. There was no way in hell Jericho was going to be okay with it. He could picture the enormous fit already. Sulking, snarking, refusing to cooperate.

"Jericho's not going to go for this at all," he muttered. "He tries to keep his family private."

"Oh, he already said it was fine. We called him yesterday afternoon."

"Seriously?"

That meant Jericho had known at dinner, and during the movies. Kerry blushed. Tara raised her eyebrows at him.

"He said it wouldn't be a problem."

"*Jesus.*"

"I can't believe I'm here," Kerry breathed. He'd picked out the resort himself when he was setting the trip up, but it didn't make it seem any more real.

Turks and Caicos. Not exactly on his list of expectations for the year. Or even his twenties. Hell, maybe not ever, although a boy could dream, and clearly those dreams came true.

They were in literal paradise.

The water was light turquoise and clear to the ground, the sky was bright and blue, and the sand was pale and warm but not hot. Kerry never ever wanted to leave. They'd gone for a secluded resort rather than something flashy and crowded. He and Jericho had a cabin near the beach, with its own catering and a private pool. They had to pose for some pap shots that would look so very genuine as long as nobody stopped to think about why there were paps on a secluded beach, but they'd look romantic. Hell, Kerry *felt* romantic.

He'd just about passed out when he saw their bungalow. It was all teak and white flowing linen, surrounded by lush vegetation on three sides with a striking view of the beach from the fourth. Their pool was hidden by tall shoots of bamboo and banana leaves, and the deck featured a stairway right down to it.

Kerry barely knew what to look at.

Except the one large bed.

He assumed he'd be sleeping on the couch. Or else… well, he didn't know what to think after the past few days. More kisses, but nothing else. They slept in their own rooms, nothing changed other than the kissing. He was honestly pretty damn confused.

"You want to hit the beach?" Jericho asked. "We aren't taking any pictures until tomorrow, so we might as well get a little bit of a tan with whatever sun is left for today," he said.

Neither of them had been seen around town for a few days before the trip. It hadn't been explicitly stated, but Kerry had the feeling they were going to make it look a lot longer than the four days they were going to be there.

"Sure. I'd love to swim."

He rarely got to go to the beach at home, and this beach was so, so much better.

Jericho rooted around in his bags for a suit and then went for the bathroom. Kerry changed quickly into his own trunks before Jericho came back out. He was sitting on the bed waiting when Jericho emerged in the trunks Kerry had seen him in back at home.

"Sunblock?" Kerry asked.

"I should be okay. It's late afternoon. I doubt we'll get burnt."

True. Of course Kerry of the lily-white, pale-ass skin didn't get to take that chance. He still sprayed on a good layer of sunscreen before he followed Jericho out the door of their bungalow.

The beach was something out of a dream—quiet, small and crescent shaped, brushed with the palest of sand and a smattering of pink shells. Kerry thought he might have landed on another planet. It was summer in LA, and had been unbearably hot, but there was a different quality to the air and the ocean, softer somehow. He wanted to touch everything, inhale the sweet floral air, dip his toes in the water, and never ever go home. Too bad they didn't have very long.

"What are you waiting for?" Jericho grinned at him.

"Nothing." Kerry dropped his towel and ran for the water, laughing.

Jericho chased after him, and they splashed into the warm water nearly at the same time. Kerry tripped over his own feet and plunged into the sea but came up still laughing. He had salt in his nose, his eyes stung because he didn't get to close them in time, and he was the happiest he'd been in a long, long time.

Jericho splashed him, and he splashed back.

"You're the mostly dry one. You want to start that game?"

Jericho rolled his eyes fondly. Fond. Kerry still couldn't believe how far they'd come from sullen and uncooperative. "Please."

Kerry didn't even think before he leaped onto Jericho and pulled him into the water. That started a splashing and wrestling war that didn't end until they were both breathless and laughing and covered with saltwater and sticky sand.

"It's so beautiful here," Kerry mused when he took a breath. The sky was starting to turn orange as the sun dipped into the ocean from where it had been hovering right above it. He stared off at the horizon. Jericho pulled him close so Kerry's back was to his front. He didn't say much but wrapped his arms around Kerry's waist and kissed his neck.

"It never looks like this at home," Kerry said. "It's almost like a different sun."

"I know what you mean." Jericho kissed him in return and twined their fingers together.

Kerry wondered if Jericho could feel how hard his heart was beating.

"Hey, what do you want for dinner tonight?"

"You're always thinking about food," Kerry grumbled to cover up his nerves. Jericho's skin was so warm and wet against his; they'd never touched shirtless before.

"Who isn't?" Jericho asked.

Good point. "What time is it even at home?" Kerry asked. It felt like a hundred years since he'd eaten, but he was so excited to be there it hadn't really occurred to him.

Jericho shrugged. "I don't really feel like figuring it out. Tell me what you want."

"Is there a menu or something?"

He grinned. "Nah. Just… pick something."

"How do we even do that?"

"We call the kitchen. They'll make pretty much anything as long as the ingredients aren't too unusual."

"Seriously."

Kerry couldn't imagine that kind of luxury, even after everything he'd seen. "I have no idea where to start. You might need to pick tonight. I'm mentally exhausted by the prospect."

Jericho nipped at his neck. "I think I can do that."

KERRY didn't know what to say when he wandered up the stairs and out to the main deck after a short nap on one of the squishy pool chairs. Jericho was nowhere to be seen, but a white billowing pavilion sat right on the beach where they'd been lounging earlier. Candles flickered everywhere, and huge torches were anchored in the sand. Kerry's breath caught in his throat—that was until he saw Jericho walk out from behind the pale curtains.

He'd changed from his swim trunks while Kerry had slept, and was dressed in khaki shorts and a thin white button-down that he hadn't bothered to button at all. He looked gorgeous. Cover-model gorgeous. Kerry wondered for a moment if their little photo shoot had been moved up a day, but there wasn't any equipment. Nothing but Jericho and a setting out of some sort of tropical fairy tale. Jericho noticed him watching.

"Come down," he called with a wave. "Dinner is here."

"I need to shower," Kerry told him.

"Later. It'll get cold."

Kerry felt a bit grimy from the airplane, the swimming, and the nap, but he shrugged into a Henley and walked down to where the dinner of his dreams was set out on a picnic blanket on the sand.

"What is all this?" he asked in a whisper.

Jericho grinned. "They brought this setup with the dinner. It's pretty romance novel, isn't it?"

"I feel like I'm in a movie."

Jericho chuckled. "Come on. Let's eat some dinner. I'm starving. I was about to come wake you up."

They ate delicious lobster and a rice dish, salads and rolls, and a mango-and-passion-fruit cake for dessert. It was all topped off by sweet pale wine and easy conversation. They laughed and teased each other. Kerry smiled more than he remembered ever smiling before in his life, but below the smile was this *tension.* He noticed Jericho. Of course he did. Jericho had miles of bronzed skin and a glamorous smile and Kerry knew how hot his kisses were, so, yeah, of course he noticed him. He had been noticing him for weeks.

But there was more under the smiles and the laughter, the impulse to reach out and run his finger down satiny skin, how he had to stop himself from climbing into Jericho's lap, unbuttoning his shorts, tasting all the skin he hadn't seen yet. Kerry wanted it. He wanted it all.

Jericho cleared his throat. "You think you're done with the wine?" he asked. His voice sounded a bit choked. Kerry wished he had more experience. He didn't know what he was meant to do next.

"Um, yeah. All done. Do we put this stuff away?"

"No. They'll come for it." Jericho's smile seemed a bit easier. He stood and held out his hand for Kerry. "Ready to head inside for the night?"

"Yeah. Okay. Let's go in."

AFTER they got inside, they took turns in the shower. Kerry took his time washing and trying to get it together before he looked like a huge inexperienced moron. He came out to find Jericho lounging on the bed in a pair of boxer shorts.

"Um, I can…." Kerry gestured toward the couch, which had to be comfortable.

"Kerry, no." Jericho murmured. "You're not sleeping on the couch. Come here."

"Are you sure?"

Jericho gave him a lazy bedroom kind of smile that made Kerry's heart race. "I'm very sure."

Kerry sat on the bed and then turned and slid under the covers. He turned to face Jericho.

"Um, hi."

Um, hi? Can I be any more awkward? His heart was pounding like every cliché of the inexperienced wallflower with the guy who was way out of his league.

Jericho grinned at him. "Hey."

Kerry knew he was blushing. *Damn it.* He didn't know what to say, but he knew he wanted to touch Jericho. Badly. Jericho's chest was bronzed and sculpted and beautiful, and *hell* he'd never wanted to touch anyone so badly in his entire life. He reached out a little, but his hand was trembling, so he snatched it back and hid it under the covers. It was Jericho—they'd spent weeks together, they'd kissed and touched and cuddled—but Kerry felt like it was all completely new. He bit his lip.

"Hey, Kerry," Jericho murmured.

"Yeah?" Kerry looked up and realized that Jericho had caught him staring. He wondered if he should go sleep on the beach. Less embarrassing.

"Come here."

Jericho reached out and pulled Kerry over to him. Their bare chests brushed together and Kerry shivered. Jericho kissed him like he had been for days. He was such an incredible kisser. Kerry rarely stopped to think about it—okay, he never did, not when he was in the moment and ready to dissolve with pleasure.

Jericho ran his fingers up and down Kerry's back and slid them inside his thin pajama bottoms. "I want you," he whispered. "I have for weeks."

"Yeah?" Kerry swallowed hard. He couldn't imagine anything he wanted more than to have Jericho inside him. It had been so long since he'd been that close to anyone, but Jericho seemed right. "I want it too."

Jericho bit his lip and then dove in for another kiss. He rolled them so Kerry was on the bottom, and Jericho's thigh was between his. Kerry rode Jericho's thigh for long minutes, kissing and touching until they were both moaning with pleasure.

"Can I take these off?" Jericho asked. He pulled at the elastic waist of Kerry's pants.

"Yes." Kerry lifted his hips and helped Jericho take the pajamas off. Then he pushed his still-trembling hands under Jericho's waistband and rid him of his boxer briefs as well.

"Are you okay?" Jericho asked.

Kerry felt the odd impulse to giggle. Great time to develop a new reaction to nerves. "Yeah. Just… you're a bit out of my league, aren't you?"

"*No*," Jericho growled. He leaned over and sucked a mark into Kerry's neck. It was rather aggressive, and Kerry liked it a lot more than he would've thought. "When will you figure out how beautiful you are?"

"I'm—"

"Yes. You are."

They kissed some more, with nothing between them. Kerry felt Jericho grow hard against his thigh, and he ground up and wrapped a leg around Jericho's hips. He wanted the pressure of fingers opening him up. He'd gone past nerves to a simmering heat that was close to boiling over. He pulled lightly on Jericho's hair.

"Do you have anything with you?" Kerry asked. It hadn't been something he'd thought of bringing.

"I do." Jericho looked a little embarrassed that he'd thought ahead, but he rolled off the bed and walked, naked, to his bag to pull out a bottle of lube and some condoms. He really was beautiful, Kerry thought. He rarely got a chance just to look. Jericho moved like one of the big cats, all sinew, supple skin, and grace. He raked his hair off his forehead and crawled back on the bed, tossing the condoms onto the bedside table but popping the lid off the lube.

Kerry lay back on the bed and let his legs fall open. He couldn't wait for Jericho to touch him. Jericho slicked his fingers and crawled beneath Kerry's thighs. He sucked kisses into the flesh there and dragged his wet, slick fingers until they were nudging against Kerry's hole.

"Yes," Kerry whispered. It had been a long time since anyone was down there but himself. He couldn't wait to feel the thickness of Jericho's fingers.

Jericho nudged in one, then a second, found Kerry's prostate and massaged it for long minutes of pleasure until Kerry felt himself unraveling.

"I'm seriously going to come if you don't stop that," Kerry muttered. It was hard for him to talk, even. He wanted more.

"Yeah?" Jericho rubbed more and licked the underside of Kerry's near-painful erection.

"Jesus. Please come up here."

"You want me to fuck you?" Jericho asked quietly.

Kerry barked out a hysterical laugh. "Before I lose my mind, *yes*. I can't believe this is happening," he added quietly.

Jericho chuckled himself, and Kerry thought the sound was a little breathy. Then he reached for the box of condoms and fished one out with slippery fingers.

"Here. Let me."

Kerry opened the condom and rolled it down Jericho's straining cock. Jericho sucked in a breath. Then Kerry hiked his legs up Jericho's hips and pulled him closer until the tip of Jericho's cock was right there, slipping inside.

"Oh, *God*." It was a little tight at first, but it was so damn good. Kerry undulated his hips and tried to get more of Jericho inside. Finally Jericho's hips were flush against him.

They were connected in so many ways—Jericho inside of him, arms bracketing his head, as they kissed breathlessly, and Kerry rubbed his thigh on Jericho's hip.

"You feel so good," Jericho choked out. He laughed breathlessly. "That was—*fuck.* Everyone says that I know. I just…."

He looked like he was in awe. Kerry pulled him close for another kiss.

From there on, it was nothing but sensation, heat and pressure and pleasure winding up inside of Kerry until he couldn't take it anymore and came harder than he remembered coming in his entire life. Jericho shouted out only moments after and stilled on top of him before he collapsed into a sweaty heap.

Kerry felt giddy and sated, shivery and hot. "That was amazing," he breathed.

"You have no idea."

CHARLESTON still felt like home. It probably always would no matter how many years Jericho spent living other places. Even though he was exhausted from their early flight and still sort of on West Coast time, he was very happy to see familiar places, the ones he'd grown up around.

His family lived on a secluded side street lined with old oak trees and bougainvillea. Jericho was a little bit hesitant for Kerry to see the house he grew up in—it wasn't exactly small. Jericho Knox hadn't come from a humble background. He figured Kerry already had the picture with the rest of the homes they'd passed, but it was always a little nerve-racking to bring someone home. Always—Jericho really wouldn't know about "always" since this was the first time he'd done it. Somehow it felt right for Kerry to meet his family, though. Like it was meant to be.

His house was like the others, three stories, soaring pillars, shutters, verandas that spanned the entire front of the house, surrounded by palmettos and an expansive lawn and garden. They'd painted it white with classic black shutters and a red door. Even though it felt like home to Jericho, he knew it was impressive to outside eyes. He only hoped Kerry didn't mind.

"Did you buy your parents this house after you were famous?" Kerry asked as their car pulled down the drive. His eyes were wide. As nice as his LA house was, it wasn't impressive like home, didn't have that stately Southern feel, the long tree-lined drive, or the huge façade.

Jericho kind of loved that Kerry assumed he'd paid for the whole thing—which he would've if there'd been a need for him to do so. Of course, that also meant he was going to have to confess that no, he didn't. Jericho cleared his throat.

"No. I grew up in this house." He blushed. Actually blushed.

Kerry let out a surprised chuckle. "Must've been nice. Jesus."

"I'd love to have some sob story about how my parents were never home and I was raised by the butler or something, but it really was nice." Jericho shrugged. "My family is close. My mom never worked. My dad just happens to be a very successful lawyer and bought this house when it was in bad shape, according to them. I've only seen pictures from before it was fixed up. Sometimes I wish I'd stayed here and followed him into the law firm. Life would be a lot easier, I think."

"That means you'd have missed out on the joys of fake dating me," Kerry joked. "How could you live without my sunny face first thing in the morning?"

"Hey. You're the best part of all of this."

He froze when he saw his mom waiting in the drive and then nearly jumped out before the cab even pulled to a complete stop. It felt like forever since he'd seen his family. Jericho put his hand on the handle of the door, but then remembered he wasn't alone. He had to help Kerry out like the Southern gentleman he was—at least in front of his mother—and introduce him.

Kerry chuckled as if he could see Jericho's dilemma. "Go. Say hi to your mom. I'll be fine."

Jericho hopped out of the car as fast as he could and wrapped his arms around his mom's shoulders. It had been months since he'd seen her—Christmas actually—but she looked good. Healthy. Jericho knew he got his eyes and his cheekbones from her, but her hair was sandy and streaked with gray instead of dark like his and his dad's. She was dressed well, like always, and she smelled like home. Jericho decided then and there that he was going to buy a house in Charleston and come home more often. Maybe sell the one in Topanga and come back to the place he felt grounded when he wasn't up in Canada filming—get a condo in LA for when he needed to be there or something.

"I missed you, Mama," Jericho whispered.

"I missed you too, baby. I'm glad you're here, even if we don't get you for very long." She looked over Jericho's shoulder. "So this is Kerry?"

Kerry stood shyly by the side. His dark hair shone in the sun, and he smiled like he wasn't sure what he was supposed to do.

"Ker, come here." Jericho chuckled and waved him over. "This is my mom Caroline. Mom, this is Kerry."

Kerry went to give her his hand, but she opened her arms for a hug. "We're huggers in this house," she said. And then gave him a kiss on the cheek. "Thank you for helping my son." Jericho noticed his cousin, Madison, peeking out the screen door at them. She had a smirk on her face as usual, and her dark hair was piled on her head in a huge bun. People had thought he and Maddie were twins growing up. They still looked an awful lot alike. Jericho was happy to see her, but…. "Mama. Why is Maddie at the house?" There was no reason for them to be over on a random weekend morning. Unless….

His mom flushed. "The family was curious about Kerry. And you told me I couldn't tell what was really going on, so what was I supposed to do when they heard he was going to be in town?"

Jericho groaned. "Not *tell* them we were going to be in town?" He looked at Kerry, whose forehead was wrinkled. Poor guy looked a little stressed out. "How many of them are here?" Jericho asked.

"Um, just Patsy and Jo and Maddie, and, well, I couldn't not invite Mama, so… everyone."

"Jesus."

"How many people is everyone?" Kerry whispered.

"A lot."

"I made brunch," his mom said quickly.

Jericho couldn't help smiling. "That does help." He looked down at Kerry. "I'm really sorry about this. I didn't expect you to have to meet my entire extended family."

"It's okay. They won't be here tomorrow, will they? You know, for the photographers."

"Nah. Most of them live in walking distance. They'll go home in a couple of hours." He gave his mom a pointed look. "Right?"

"Yes. They'll go home."

JERICHO led Kerry into the house, where there was a huge brunch set up, and yes, every single one of his family members. "Brace yourself," he whispered. He loved his family, but they were big and loud and Southern, and he didn't know if Kerry had ever experienced anything quite like them. Aunts and uncles and cousins surrounded them and smothered both of them with hugs and kisses and congratulations.

"Um, guys. I'm sure you're starving, and you want to eat. Let me show Kerry up to my room so we can put our stuff away."

He got a few whistles from Maddie, who was not only his cousin but one of his closest friends. Jericho felt bad lying to her. She'd known all the girls were fake, of course, since she'd been the first one Jericho came out to back when they were about thirteen. But everyone seemed to be buying Kerry. Nobody had given them a single searching stare like they weren't quite buying the romance. Jericho decided it was best not to think about why.

He took Kerry's bag and gestured for him to lead up the grand staircase in the middle of the foyer where his family was still gathered.

"Y'all can go eat anytime," Jericho called out to the crowd. "We're not going to do anything entertaining in the next five minutes." They chuckled but started shuffling to the dining room to grab plates.

As soon as he and Kerry were at the top of the stairs, Jericho let out a long sigh. "I am so sorry. I should've known this would happen. I have the nosiest family in the history of the world. I love them, but there wasn't a chance that they'd leave this alone."

"No, it's fine. They seem sweet."

Jericho laughed. "Famous last words."

THE day had been exhausting but really pretty amazing at the same time. It was just like he remembered, having the whole family around, joking and laughing, and telling embarrassing stories. He shouldn't have worried about Kerry. Kerry melted into them like he'd always been there. Jericho knew he should probably be worried about how he saw Kerry in the corner whispering with Maddie, but it was all so great he had a hard time caring. Jericho couldn't stop smiling. He was *happy*. In the middle of a bullshit publicity stunt, lying to a huge chunk of his family, he was happy.

Jericho found his mom in the kitchen putting away the rest of the dinner dishes with their housekeeper Rose's help. He came up behind her and hugged her gently. He kissed her on the cheek.

"Hey, Mama. Today was wonderful. Thank you for putting all of that together." Jericho would've thought it would be a nightmare to plunk Kerry into his gigantic Labrador puppy pile of a family. But Kerry seemed to honestly love being with them. He'd played the doting boyfriend with Jericho like he was meant for the part. Jericho was starting to wonder how much of their relationship was an act and how much was very much for real.

"I'm glad you had fun. Kerry is an absolute darling. This is the happiest I've seen you in years." His mother turned and kissed him on the cheek.

"Ma, you know Kerry isn't really my fiancé. He's just helping me get through the scandal, and we're friends. We get along."

"Of course, dear." Caroline snickered. "That's about the opposite from what your face says when you look at him—and his face when he looks at you. That boy is falling for you, and if I know my son, you're falling for him right back."

Jericho stared at his mom for a long moment. "Are you serious?" he asked.

"Am I wrong?" Caroline Knox raised one perfectly groomed eyebrow.

Jericho had never been able to lie to her, as much as he'd wished he could back when he was in school and trying to sneak in late. Damn.

"No. You're not wrong. Not on my end at least." Jericho sighed. "I didn't mean to feel like this. It's not good timing. I don't even know when it happened."

He wasn't even sure when he admitted it to himself. Probably not many seconds before he admitted it to his mom. He was falling for Kerry. For real. He was falling hard.

"Just give it time, baby." She cupped his face. "I know you two had an... unconventional start, but I think this could really mean something."

"Maybe you're right."

"Plus," she said with a grin, "the hardest part has been done already, now, hasn't it?"

"What's that?" Jericho asked.

"The whole world already thinks you two are in love. You've braved the coming out, you've shown the whole world your relationship. Now all you have to do is follow through and be the person you've been in public."

Just that easy, huh? Jericho smiled. "I'm beat. I think I'm going to go up and go to bed. Kerry passed out practically the second we sat down."

"Okay. Night baby. It's good to have you here again."

Jericho was quiet for a moment. "You know, I've been thinking of buying a place down here. Coming home a lot more often. I miss how I feel when I'm here, and I think it's better for me than LA."

That sentence sounded like home and family. Especially because when Jericho pictured it in his head, Kerry was all of a sudden with him, smiling and hugging family and at barbecues and brunches and visiting him in Vancouver…. *Damn*.

"I'd love that. You know I would." His mom gave him another one of her knowing smiles. "I'll see you in the morning. I'll try to let you two kids sleep in. I know you're probably worn out."

"Thanks. Night, Mama. Tell Pops night too. I bet he's out in the woodshop."

"For at least another hour. I'll tell him."

JERICHO crept up the stairs and found Kerry sprawled on his belly on Jericho's childhood bed—good thing he'd grown up sleeping on a huge four poster queen. Two adult men were not meant to share a twin. Jericho chuckled under his breath and stripped out of his jeans and shirt. Then he brushed his teeth and crawled into the bed next to a sleeping Kerry. Kerry woke and rolled over.

"Hey. What time is it?" Kerry's voice was slurred and gravelly. Jericho thought he sounded adorable.

"It's barely eleven, you high roller. I'm beat too, though."

"Did you have a good talk with your mom?" Kerry asked.

"Yes. She loves you, by the way."

Kerry rolled over and put his face in Jericho's neck. It felt safe and intimate. Jericho loved it. He threaded his fingers through Kerry's hair and massaged the back of his head.

"I'm sorry I met her like this, even if she knows the truth. I feel bad about your family."

"I know. But…." Jericho wasn't ready to say it, to jump into the place where he asked Kerry if they were real. It sure as hell felt real. The night in the cabin felt real, meeting his family, cuddling in his old bed like they were meant to be there with not a single person watching or taking pictures. It felt like a relationship.

Jericho leaned forward and kissed Kerry. It started slow but deepened until Kerry was groaning in his mouth. Kerry finally pulled away with a laugh.

"What?" Jericho wanted to kiss him more. He'd gotten addicted to Kerry's body on the island. It had been hours since they'd been naked together. He slid his hands down Kerry's back and under the waistband of his pajama pants.

"I'm so not going to do this in your family's house with your parents still *awake*."

"No sense of adventure," Jericho said. "I'm appalled."

Kerry laughed and attacked him with a violent smattering of kisses.

Chapter Ten

KERRY didn't want to leave Charleston. There was something about the old town that felt like home. Part of it was Caroline and the way she'd welcomed him like he was her own son, even though he knew Jericho had told her the truth. But it was just… different. Everything was different, first the island, and then getting to see what Jericho was really like with his family and loved ones around. Kerry had always worried that he'd been getting in too far, and he knew it. He was in all the way. It was too late to do anything about it. Sometime between the first time they'd kissed for real with nobody watching, and the morning he'd woken up in Jericho's childhood bed with Jericho curled around him like a content spouse, Kerry's whole heart had clicked into place. It felt right with them together. Like it was meant to be that way.

He was falling in love. Fast. Kerry just hoped he wasn't in for a world of heartbreak.

They took a cab to the airport that afternoon. He watched Charleston go from the window of the car.

"It's really amazing here," Kerry finally said. "I wish we didn't have to leave."

Jericho reached over and took his hand. "I'm glad you liked it. I can't believe how much Mama loves you." Jericho chuckled. "Says you're the best thing that's ever happened to me."

"Not your big fancy career?" Kerry asked.

"No. She actually hates that."

"She knows it wasn't… me in that picture, right?" Kerry loved Caroline so much. He hated the thought of her thinking he was that kind of guy.

"Yeah. But she also knows it definitely was me." Jericho closed his eyes like he really didn't want to think about the picture. Kerry didn't blame him.

"Sorry. I didn't mean…."

"It's okay. We all make mistakes. I've just made more than most. Believe me."

"Things are looking up for you, though."

They'd gotten e-mail confirmation from Tom that Jericho was in for the role and they'd made the final decision that they weren't going to recast. The producers were happy with the way he'd turned the whole club situation around and were ready to sign him as a permanent cast member.

Jericho looked over at him. "They're definitely looking up."

Kerry slept though most of the flight, not that he was particularly tired, but there was something about airplanes that always made him fall asleep and stay there. When he woke, they were landing in LAX.

"You ready to face the music?" Jericho asked.

"Not till tomorrow," Kerry groaned. "Can't we just have one more relaxing night?"

"Oh, there is no chance they didn't make sure the paps knew we were coming. It's time to sing for our supper."

Kerry knew exactly what the paps at LAX were like when someone like Jericho came through the public exit. He'd analyzed enough footage to know it was like throwing chum in a shark tank.

"Is it too much to ask that we sneak out the back?"

"You think George would like that? He's going to want us tanned and in love right in front of the paparazzi. That was partly the point of all of this, wasn't it?"

"I hate George," Kerry grumbled. "Let me at least go do something with my hair. I have seat head." He was sure his hair was scrunched up in the back and ratted from the long flight.

"Sure thing."

THE flashes were intense, like they always were. Kerry doubted in the short time he had left in the spotlight that he'd ever get used to it. He wondered if lifers like Jericho really did. It was kind of sad to think of in a way, that having people examine every move he made started to feel normal. Maybe that was why he liked it so much in Charleston—everyone in town knew who he was and they kind of left him alone out of respect. He'd gotten smiles and waves, but that was about it. Kerry felt bad that they'd brought photographers there.

At least they'd been in and out and left them alone the rest of the trip.

They slid into the waiting car, and Kerry dropped his head against the cool leather seat.

"I can't believe I actually thought you liked that at first. I thought you were a fame seeker."

"Yes, the meek PR stooge secretly wants to be Paris Hilton."

"Not Britney?" Jericho raised his eyebrows.

"Okay. Maybe. At the very least I should've been on *The Hills*."

"Nah, you're better than that. You deserve at least one music video and a spot on a competition show. *Dancing with the Stars*?"

Kerry dissolved into giggles at the thought of him trying to dance.

"Probably better stay away from that one."

They chatted all the way back to the house, spent a quiet evening with dinner and a dip in the pool, and then slid into bed early, since both of them were acclimated to East Coast time. Kerry had turned for his own room when they'd decided to head to sleep, but Jericho laced their fingers together and tugged him toward the spiral stairs. "*Stay with me*," he'd whispered.

Kerry had nodded silently, heart in his throat, and followed Jericho to his huge, airy room.

"What time do you have to get up?" Jericho rumbled from where he was curled around Kerry's back. It already felt right to be there with Jericho in his space. Kerry turned and faced Jericho.

"Fuck. Early. I'll set my alarm."

"Tell George to suck it. You need a day off."

"This whole week was a day off," Kerry reminded him with a chuckle. "Plus, who do you think sets most of this stuff up and makes sure the pictures and press releases get to the right places? I have work to do."

"Please. Don't even pretend you weren't dealing with e-mails and stuff on your phone. Plus, while it was fun, this was all for the publicity thing. In a way, it was definitely work."

"Okay. Yeah. But it was still really great."

"It was."

Kerry eventually detangled himself from Jericho and crawled over to his phone to set the alarm for six. Six. Sounded like the pits of hell. Then he let Jericho cuddle him back in, and in no time at all, Kerry felt himself falling asleep.

THE morning was painful, but not as bad as it usually was since they'd gone to bed at granny time, basically. He struggled out of Jericho's bed, down the stairs and into the shower before he shoved some breakfast in his mouth and headed to the office. Everyone was there when he arrived; there wasn't such a thing as a late start for George Jones. Kerry headed straight to his desk but was quickly ambushed by Tara.

"You look gorgeous. And happy."

"It was a fun week. Not so excited to be back here."

"Babe. Do we need to have a talk about Jericho Knox?" Tara asked.

"No." Kerry was sure he blushed. Maybe his tan would be enough to cover it up at least a little. "Why?"

"Because you have a fading hickey just below the collar of your shirt, and I know he didn't give it to you when the photographers were there."

"Oh." Kerry didn't know how he was supposed to respond to that. He remembered getting it very well.

Jericho deep inside him, biting and sucking at the base of his neck. He had to bite his lip to keep from groaning.

"Yes. Oh." Tara gave him a knowing look. "Be careful, babycakes. I know you know that, but just… be careful."

"I'm not being stupid. I promise."

Not exactly the truth. Especially if falling for the client was under the stupid category.

"You're never stupid, babe. Just… you know."

"I know."

OSCAR came up to Kerry's desk. "Hey, I need to talk to you about the Tanya Ivanov shoot next week. She's balking at the idea of going through with the whole pap walk at the restaurant scenario, but it's the best thing. She likes you. Can you talk to her?"

"She told me she's worried about the crowds. She's a tiny girl, Oscar, and she's always had anxiety. It would be scary. It is scary. I know."

Oscar rolled his eyes. "Look at you, Mister Celebrity. Looks like you've already forgotten that when the sheen of Jericho Knox wears off of you, you'll be just like you were before. A big nobody."

Oscar walked away.

Tara flipped him off. "Seriously. I'm going to talk to Abby about getting rid of that tool."

"Ignore him. I know he wanted this job with Jericho. I bet he really would've even dyed his hair to do it. Maybe I should've let him take it if his panties were going to get so twisted over the whole thing."

Tara giggled. "Can you picture Oscar making out with Jericho? It's so *wrong*."

It only took Kerry a few seconds to get over the shot of intense jealousy before he saw the humor in it. "Yeah. Besides, I think Jericho would chew him up and spit him out before lunch."

"You're probably right."

KERRY hadn't spent so much time naked in his entire life, let alone naked, sweaty, and sated with a beautiful man draped on top of him. He dragged his palm down Jericho's sweaty back and stretched a little to test how sore he was—which was considerably after last night and the nice little wake-up call he'd just gotten.

"I never want to leave this bed," Jericho moaned. "Can we just stay here all day tomorrow? I'll let you work. I'll even order pizza—that veggie kind you like and all."

While he'd managed to drag himself in all week even though every day felt harder than the last, it was Friday. And he didn't want to do it.

Kerry shrugged. "What are they going to do to me if I call in? Fire me?" He kind of did have George by the balls, and while he knew it would be stupid to play fast and loose with his current position, one mental health day couldn't be that bad. He'd just had to live through the stress of meeting the fam. Sure it had been great and comfortable and like going to his own home, and he'd already had four days to recover, but George didn't need to know everything was fine and easy.

"You know what? I'll e-mail Abby. Tell her I'm feeling a bit under the weather. There isn't much going on today."

"Will she believe you?" Jericho asked.

"Does it really matter?"

Jericho chuckled. "I think I'm wearing off on you. Pretty soon we'll have you drinking too much and riding a hog."

"The hog is so not going to happen." Kerry cringed. "Sexy on you. A disaster waiting to happen for me."

"I should take you out on it. Maybe after dinner." Jericho tickled him a little.

"I'm sick, remember?"

Jericho chuckled. "I think if the paps get us on a romantic couple's motorcycle ride, you'll be forgiven for your fake cold. And if they don't? Well, then, nobody has to know."

Kerry grinned. "You are rubbing off on me."

"Wouldn't mind doing more of the rubbing."

"Insatiable." Kerry pushed at Jericho, but then he ended up grinning and nuzzling into Jericho's neck. It was really nice. The day was bright, but they all were in the middle of an LA summer, and he didn't feel the need to get out into the sun. He liked their cozy nest. Kerry whipped out his laptop before he could forget and shot an e-mail to Abby with George copied about not feeling well. He never took days off. He was past due. They actually did get out of bed to go downstairs and make some breakfast. They had scrambled eggs with basil and gouda cheese, turkey bacon, and some of Jericho's ridiculously expensive coffee.

"I don't know how I'm going to go back to office coffee after this," Kerry muttered. "This stuff should be illegal."

He noticed Jericho give him a strange look out of the corner of his eye, but he brushed it aside.

"Ready for bed and lazy time?" Jericho asked.

"Definitely."

Kerry figured they'd last an hour or so, then maybe watch a movie or swim in the pool, but just the thought of sleeping in when he knew he should be at work made him quiver happily. It was like magic—the magic of not doing a damn thing and having the guy he... well *the guy* in bed with him. Kerry raced up the stairs behind Jericho, followed him into his room, and did a flying leap onto his high white bed.

"Do you do this a lot? Stay in your bed and sleep in?"

Jericho shook his head. "When I'm on a show, we have early set times. When I'm not? Well, Tom usually has something he needs me to do. Or the trainer comes."

"I haven't seen a trainer since I've been here," Kerry said.

Jericho shrugged. "He's been around. Usually when you're at work. That's kind of my job, you know."

Kerry reached out and squeezed Jericho's bicep. "Looking like a hot cop?"

"Yeah. At least I know I'll have one fan."

He leaned over and gave Kerry a kiss. Then he pulled back with the softest smile Kerry had ever seen. He was so... nice. Sweet almost, and genuine and friendly and goofy. Kerry just stared.

"What?" Jericho asked.

"Nothing."

"Why are you staring at me?"

"I don't know. Still trying to figure you out I guess. I figured out a long time ago that you weren't really your image."

"I was starting to become that guy, so yeah. I kind of was."

Kerry looked for another few long silent moments. "But you didn't feel like him. Not really."

"No. Not really. I guess it hadn't taken me very long away from that life to realize that's not who I was meant to be."

"What were you like back at home growing up?"

Jericho groaned. "Do we really have to discuss this? I'm sure my mom told you plenty."

"Not with words. She'd protect you from anything, including a nosy... me." He didn't know what word to say. Fake boyfriend who you're sleeping with? Yeah, that sounded pretty awkward. "The only things I learned from her were from her actions. From the way she treated you, the way you treated her and the rest of your family. It was like leather-jacketed, hog-riding Jericho Knox disappeared."

"Yeah. My mom really hates reading shit about me and what my life is like here." Jericho reached over and brushed Kerry's hair off his face. "You know, she said you were the best thing that happened to me since I left home. And the leaving is not on her list of good. She really likes you. She's called me twice this week to talk about it." Jericho chuckled.

"I really like her too. Are you dodging my question?"

"Kind of."

"*Jericho.*"

"Jay. I'm sure you heard everyone at home call me that. You should too."

Kerry's heart did an odd little pitter-patter at that. "Jay, then. What were you like as a kid? I have to know. I know you said you were happy with your family, but what about the rest?"

He buried his face into the pillow and groaned out a few words Kerry couldn't make out.

"What?"

"I was a gigantic nerd, okay? No. Not gigantic. I was a skinny, short, acne-ridden nerd. I don't really like to talk about it."

"You?" Kerry nearly squealed. "That might be the cutest thing I've ever heard. Badass Jericho was a nerd."

"Yes. And that information will go literally no farther than this bed. I've spent a lot of time shutting down people from Charleston who remember how geeky I was. It's not a cute story. Luckily most of the kids from my high school don't remember me at all." His face clouded for a moment like there was more to the story than that. "They like to tell anyone who will listen that they went to school with me, but if they're pressed to come up with a story of our time together, they can't."

"That's…."

"Better that way. Believe me. Rather be the quiet kid they don't remember than… I don't know. Someone they have lots to say about."

"I guess."

"Hey. No more nerd talk. What were you like in high school?"

Kerry laughed. "A nerd. Did you really expect anything else?"

"Head cheerleader?"

"Right." Kerry rolled his eyes.

"What was Cole like in high school?"

Kerry rolled his eyes again. "Cole." He sometimes wondered how he and his brother had gotten to be best friends. "Okay. Like you said. No more nerd talk."

"Cool." Jericho leaned in and kissed Kerry long and deep. Kerry figured it was his way of shutting them up. Kerry was all for it.

JERICHO was in so deep, and he had no idea how to get out. He didn't even know if he wanted to get out. He and Kerry spent the rest of the morning in bed. They didn't even have sex, and Jericho, while he would never say no to more sex with Kerry, found that he liked talking to Kerry just as much as touching him.

He liked how Kerry's cheeks scrunched up when he laughed and how he bit his lip when he was embarrassed about something. They ordered pizza and watched movies, and Jericho hadn't had such a good day in a long, long time—even the one watching his family fall in love. Every day with Kerry felt more real, every minute more intimate. He was drowning in it, and he loved every second.

It sucked watching Kerry leave in the morning. Jericho had never been the guy sitting behind watching someone go to work and promising him he'd see him in a few hours. He'd never watched someone go to work at all.

He'd never woken up in bed with someone before either, at least not someone whose name he knew. Not before Kerry. But he waved, and smiled, and nodded when Kerry said he'd be home a little late because he had work to catch up on. Then he kissed him good-bye and wondered why he felt a little restless.

JERICHO wished he'd brought Kerry as soon as he got to the club that night. He'd been booked to be at this event for months; it wasn't part of their planned schedule of appearances, just something he'd always been contracted to do. He hadn't wanted to go, and

Kerry had been exhausted from a long day at work, so Jericho had gone alone. They'd asked him about Kerry on his way in, if there was trouble in paradise, why Jericho was there alone. He'd just laughed it off and said Kerry was tired from work, and he was probably already asleep. It felt weird to be somewhere without him. After only a few short months, everything felt weird without Kerry by his side.

Jericho wanted to go home.

He did the usual rounds, shook the hands, posed for pictures next to the big cut-out of whatever celebrity vodka the party was promoting, then got in line at the bar. He was going to do one hour and he'd be out. He didn't care if he had to sneak out through the kitchen; Jericho wasn't in the mood to party.

A guy jostled into him in line.

"Um, hi there," Jericho said. He knew the look of someone barely drunk enough to stand upright. He'd had it himself more than once. He gave the guy a polite smile and went to turn around again when he realized the dude was talking to him.

"Jericho Knox. Used to be the biggest badass in town," the guy slurred.

"Excuse me?" Jericho's heart stilled in his chest. His drunk neighbor looked angry for some reason. He peered at Jericho through watery red eyes like Jericho had done something to personally offend him. The guy reminded him of the boys in his high school, the ones who *hadn't* ignored him but seemed to find fault in his very existence. They were always bigger than him, like this dude, crowded his space, and said horrible things to him. Jericho had to hold back a shudder.

"I used to think you were the shit, different woman every night, hot cars, hot bike. Now look at you. Pussy whipped by some dude. Fuck. What's happening to the world when real men turn into fags?"

"Pussy!" Jericho's head slammed into the locker, the grate sliced at his skin, his vision blacked out for a minute.

Jericho felt like he was going to pass out. He thought he was over those guys. Like he'd told Kerry, he didn't like to think about school. It hadn't been pleasant. But it had been years since he'd let himself think about his past. He'd opened himself up to feel things for Kerry, though, and then suddenly they were there, banging right on his head and his memory and— he gripped the side of the bar. His palms were sweaty and they slipped; Jericho nearly fell. He breathed for a second and then got his composure back. *You're not that kid anymore.*

"Okay, I think you've had enough to drink." Jericho gestured at the security guard, one of many who were stationed in unobtrusive places to help keep the peace in a venue with no cordoned off VIP area.

The security guy helped the drunken asshole off to the side, but Jericho stood there reeling still. The words echoed in his head *pussy... fag... momma's boy....* He'd nearly landed in the hospital once or twice before his mom put a stop to it and pulled him out to finish with a tutor. He'd spent so many years trying to get over what they'd done to him, and years where his walls were so thick nobody could get through.

I shouldn't have let anyone in.

He'd forgotten how big of a mess he used to be, how much everything hurt.

Jericho decided an hour wasn't going to cut it. He'd done the rounds; he was fucking leaving. He was done.

KERRY was asleep when Jericho got home, in the bed they'd been sharing for days and days. He was curled up on his side, smiling a little bit in his sleep. Jericho watched him and felt his belly warm up, but then he remembered the taunts, and he cringed. He went into the shower, turned it on boiling hot, and stood there for a long, long time.

He couldn't go back to being that sad, battered kid. He refused to. Jericho slid into bed next to Kerry—Kerry who turned over and reached for Jericho in his sleep. Jericho shied away, curled onto his other side and stared at the wall. A warm tender part of him wanted to touch Kerry more than anything in the world, hold him, kiss him, tell him what he'd been too scared to tell him the other day.

Another part of Jericho wanted to run.

Chapter Eleven

KERRY couldn't remember the last time he'd felt like this. Probably because the answer was never. He'd never felt like this. He'd had two solid boyfriends before. Both of them were nice guys, but more comfort than heat. He'd liked them. He'd even told the second one that he loved him, but it wasn't like this. Nothing in the world was like this.

He woke up every morning and both wanted to fly out of bed because he was so happy and at the same time he wanted to stay in bed forever because that's where Jericho was. At the moment, he was halfway between the two. Jericho was asleep, wrapped around him and rubbing sleepily at his belly. He had his warm body plastered all along Kerry's back, which was obviously his favorite way to sleep, since they ended there every morning even if they'd fallen asleep in a different position.

He'd been weird that night after the vodka party Kerry had skipped. Kerry had pretended to be asleep, but he'd heard Jericho in the shower for a long time, and he'd felt him scoot away. The next morning, though, things were seemingly back to normal. And the day after that. And the day after that. Kerry had brushed it off to a bad night and forgotten it.

Jericho groaned when Kerry's phone alarm went off, but then smacked his lips a few times and fallen back to sleep.

Kerry tried to wriggle his way out from under Jericho's arm so he could get up and go to work.

"Where you going?" Jericho mumbled.

"Work. It's Monday."

They'd stayed up unfortunately late the night before. They'd done the obligatory public appearance at an industry party but left after a few pictures were taken and come home for a night of video games and beer. It had been after two when they'd finally crawled into bed. The morning was painful at best.

"Stay here."

"I can't. I skipped a day last week, and one the week before." Kerry had been less than excited about going to work ever since they'd gotten back from Charleston. It felt like the summer was slipping away. There were only days left before Jericho had to go to Vancouver and he had to go back to his regularly scheduled life. Kerry wondered what would become of him and Jericho. He wanted to bring it up, because more than anything, he didn't want them to end. He wasn't sure if that was his call, though. He wasn't the one about to leave.

"I'll call George myself. Tell him you can't come in until lunch. You stayed up too late with me last night at that event, right? You were doing your job. You shouldn't have to come in this morning as well."

"Feel free to try to convince Abby of that." *And good luck because she doesn't really consider the events work—more like a paycheck with benefits.*

"Pssh. I'll go right to George. Give me your phone."

Kerry handed over his phone with an indulgent laugh. "Please don't get me fired."

"I won't."

Jericho pulled up George's contact info and pushed send. "Hey. George. No, this is Jericho. Listen, I heard Kerry's alarm going off from the hallway, but the poor kid is passed out. He stayed out at that beach party with me last night for a long time… yeah. I know. Is it cool if he comes in this afternoon? Tomorrow? Great." Jericho winked at him.

Kerry buried his face into the pillow and started giggling. He tried to make sure it was nearly silent.

Jericho said good-bye to George and hung up the phone. "You can go in tomorrow," he said.

"I can't believe you just did that."

"Why?" Jericho laughed. "You really were working last night, and you really shouldn't have to work this morning. That's kind of fair."

Kerry flopped his whole body into Jericho's unbelievably amazing mattress. "So are we going back to sleep?"

"It's only been four hours since we got here in the first place. I vote yes."

"Me too. Give me my phone, you bad influence." Kerry took his phone back from Jericho and plugged it in. "I'd better not get in any shit because of this."

"If you do, blame it on me. I turned your alarm off and didn't wake you up. You were just so worn out from trying to deal with me. I am a pain, after all."

Kerry giggled and curled his body back into Jericho's. "You are."

HE did go to work the next day. On time and everything. The looks he got from Abby, Oscar, and Tara when he walked in said that they all knew exactly how worn out from working he'd been the other day.

"Must be tough to be you," Oscar mumbled under his breath. "I don't know how you manage your overwhelming schedule."

"Charming as usual, Oscar."

"Whatever."

He hadn't sat in his desk for long before Tara rushed over. "What on earth happened to you yesterday?"

"I was exhausted." He groaned. He hoped it sounded realistic. "Those night events really aren't my thing."

She snorted. "From my super-secret sources, I heard you were there all of twenty minutes before you and Jericho slipped out."

Kerry sighed. "Fine. But don't tattle. We ended up staying up late and playing Tekken all night, okay? I was tired. Gaming is hard work."

"You suck so hard." She still grinned at him.

"That is why I'm in this position, isn't it?" Kerry asked.

Tara took a second to get it, but then she swatted his arm. "I'm really glad your family knows that wasn't really you."

"It would've been a deal breaker for me if I couldn't tell at least Cole."

Tara nodded like she got it. "So tell me about lover boy."

"Jericho? You know him."

"I'm starting to get the feeling that I don't. The Jericho I know wouldn't have you looking like you're about to melt into a pile of lovey-dovey goo."

"Tara."

"What? You know I'm right."

"Yeah, you kind of are. But still. Can we please pretend that I've remained one hundred percent professional, and I'm not sleeping with our client."

"You're sleeping with him?"

"Jesus. Quiet. And I can't believe I just told you that." Kerry made a face. "To be quite honest, I can't believe you didn't already know."

"Why?"

"I don't know, I thought you'd figured it out already. Shit. Don't tell anybody, okay? Nobody."

"Yeah, of course. Kerry, you and Jericho Knox?"

"I know. Worst idea in history. Believe me, I know."

"So seriously. Tell me what he's like, because I know what we get can't be the real story."

Kerry felt his face melt into a sappy, soft smile. He knew that it happened because Tara burst into giggles. "Oh my God," she muttered.

"You're right. He's nothing like what you'd expect once you get to know him. Nothing at all."

FOUR nights until Jericho left. And they were spending one of them at a party, which was the last thing Kerry wanted. Still, there they were. The party was private, swanky, in a house rather than a public venue, and crawling with security. They'd left their phones at the door; no pictures were allowed inside. It wasn't part of their publicity scheme. It was just a party. Jericho had wanted Kerry to come with him. As much as he hadn't wanted to go, it had to mean something that Jericho had wanted him there. The house was huge, surrounded by a large yard and a very large fence. There was a pool, where people swam in the backlit glow of nighttime water, and it was surrounded by groups of people chatting and carrying drinks.

"Hey, I want to say hello to a few people and talk some business. Are you okay here for a while?" Jericho asked.

He didn't know anyone at all, but sure. Whatever business Jericho had to talk was probably none of his concern.

"Sure."

Kerry found a lounger and sat by the pool with his cocktail. It was a little lonely watching the rest of the party.

HE sat there for ten minutes, fifteen, twenty, thirty.... Finally Kerry decided to get up and get a drink. He'd played this game before, where he sat there and waited for Jericho to come back. He wasn't in the mood for another of Jericho's ex-flings to stop by and tell him that he didn't have a chance to make it work. He knew that, or at least he always thought he had, until the past few weeks, but he didn't want to hear it.

Kerry made his way over to the bar and waited in the short line.

"You're Kerry, aren't you?" he heard. Kerry had been used to being called "Jericho's boyfriend" at best, but someone knew his name. A stranger knew his name. He turned.

"Yeah, I'm Kerry. Hi. Have we…?" He hoped like hell he hadn't met the stunning redhead before and forgotten her.

"No. We haven't. I'm Joanne. Jericho's shot for us a couple times before, but he's like a different person these days. I've never seen him so happy. You must be good for him."

"Shot for you?"

"For my clothes line." She smiled. "I'm not usually around LA. I'm more of a New York girl. Shhhh." She winked at Kerry.

Joanne. Clothes. Red hair. Oh God. Kerry decided to pretend he hadn't just realized exactly who he was talking to. Joanne Kingsley. Huge fashion icon and the biggest of deals. He just smiled and tried to play it cool. "Thank you. I hope he's happy."

She gave him a big grin. "Definitely. I know love when I see it. Missing my own, but they decided to stay in Manhattan."

"They?" Kerry cocked his head. He knew her name, obviously, but he didn't know much about her.

"Wife and baby. She's one and she had a cold, so both my girls decided to stay on the East Coast rather than come here."

Joanne whipped out her phone. There was a picture of a gorgeous little cherub and a statuesque woman who looked like a runway model.

"You do have a beautiful family," Kerry said. "I hope you get to see them soon."

"Two days. What are you drinking?"

Kerry hadn't noticed they'd made it up to the bar. "Oh, whiskey sour, please."

She ordered his drink and her own and then handed his over. "Where's Jericho?" she asked.

"I have—"

"Right here."

Finally. It had been long enough.

"Sorry that took so long, babe." He gave Joanne a kiss on the cheek, then came up behind Kerry and wrapped his arms around him. "You two having fun?"

"We just met, actually, but your fiancé is a lovely young man. You're lucky, you sourpuss. I'm glad you finally got someone to make you smile."

"I'm not a sourpuss." Jericho chuckled.

"You are. You tortured poor Sasha at the shoot last year, don't even pretend you didn't."

Jericho shrugged. "Tell him sorry for me. Can I steal this one? I'd like to introduce him to a few people."

"Really?" Kerry asked.

Jericho gave him a quizzical look. "Of course."

He pulled Kerry away from Joanne with pleasant good-byes and another round of kisses on the cheek for both of them.

"Who do you want me to meet?" Kerry said.

"Oh, Wiley is here. He's my new costar, but we've been friends for years. He specially requested a meeting with the man who changed my entire demeanor. His words, not mine."

Kerry chuckled. "Okay."

He let Jericho lead him rather enthusiastically into the party—drag was probably more like it, but happy like a puppy. He stopped and waved at people, introduced them to Kerry, kept his arm around Kerry's shoulders, or their hands linked, and he never let him go even once. It was rather surprising after the first part of the party, where Kerry had honestly been contemplating taking a cab back to Jericho's to fall asleep.

"There he is. Wiley!"

Kerry liked Wiley immediately. He'd always had a mild crush on him as well, and who wouldn't—gorgeous jet-black curls, dark creamy skin, glamorous smile, gravelly voice—he was the stuff of dreams. He also happened to be exceedingly genuine, friendly, and very excited to meet Kerry. Kerry didn't have to wonder why everyone kept saying he'd changed Jericho so much. He'd seen the old Jericho. He'd just always assumed it was for his benefit, since Jericho had hated him. Apparently not.

They talked to Wiley for a good half hour, about the upcoming shooting season, since Wiley played a more seasoned detective to Jericho's newbie, about Wiley's wife and new baby, about the Bears and the Packers, which made Kerry yawn, and about Kerry's apparent upcoming visit to Vancouver. Which he hadn't heard one peep about, obviously.

"Oh, uh, yeah. It'll be great to see Canada. All the trees and stuff," he mumbled.

Jericho looked momentarily uncomfortable too, like he hadn't expected Wiley to bring it up. "You'll like it, babe."

Kerry, who'd actually been having a pleasant time, was right back at the point where he'd like to disappear into a cab and get out of there.

"I'm sure I will," he said quietly.

He wasn't sure if that answered his question or not, if he and Jericho would be over when he left, or maybe Jericho was just trying to save face in front of a friend. Kerry didn't know.

JERICHO felt bad for freaking out at Kerry during the party. He'd known exactly how long he was gone, and he knew it was incredibly rude. He also knew that every time he let himself feel what he was feeling, the voices came flooding back in. Jericho was right back where he'd been when he'd escaped from those guys and his school all the way to the opposite side of the country. He wanted everything about Kerry. But he didn't want to lose the walls he'd spent so many years building.

He was all over Kerry as soon as they got back to the house. It was normal again, the stomach flipping terror had subsided, and all he could feel was Kerry. Kerry's skin, his kiss, how he stripped his clothes and inhibitions and opened himself for Jericho's touch and body and love.

Jericho opened him with slick fingers, raining kisses and praise all over him, and then when it was time, he sank inside Kerry's tight heat and felt like he was whole again.

I love you....

He breathed hard and stroked in deep, like he never wanted to leave Kerry's body.

I love you....

It was hard to hold the words in when Kerry was arched beneath him, panting and moaning out his name.

And then Jericho was coming, spilling into the condom and shouting, and he heard the voices in the back of his mind.

Pussy....
Fag....

He squeezed his eyes shut and tried not to cry. Jericho wanted Kerry more than he'd ever wanted anything in his life. He wanted to let go of his past and wrap Kerry in his arms and love him as hard as he could.

He just… couldn't.

Jericho knew he had to end it.

KERRY was comfortable… an odd feeling he realized, seeing as he was wandering around a movie star's house in his sweats. But when he simply existed and forgot the strangeness of the life he'd been living for, God, nearly three months, all he could think about was Jericho's arms when he woke up spooned against him, or how they kissed when they made love, or how Jericho whispered in his ear that he'd never met anyone like him before. It was supposed to be a façade, but nothing in Kerry's life had ever felt more real.

He was alone. One of the few times he'd ever been in Jericho's house alone. Jericho was at some event that Kerry would've gone to—he was invited—but Jericho had told him it would be boring and crowded, and he wouldn't stay long. He'd seemed squirrelly when he left, so Kerry hadn't pushed it. They'd spent nearly every waking moment together, after all—maybe they both needed a minute to breathe. So he made a cup of tea and settled on the couch in the entertainment room with his laptop and the television and prepared to relax. For the first time in a long, long time, he wanted to just… melt into the background.

Of course, that's when his phone started ringing. He looked at the caller ID and slid his thumb across the screen.

"Hey, Tara Banana. What's up?"

"Don't look at Twitter," Tara said as soon as Kerry picked up the phone. Her voice was clipped and so different than her usual giggles and smiles.

"You can't be serious. Like you're going to call here and say that and I'm not going to look."

"I am serious. Please, don't get on Twitter, don't check your mentions, don't… just don't."

What the hell happened? Kerry did exactly what Tara told him not to do—which irony was, had she not called, he probably would've stayed off Twitter anyway. It had never been his favorite part of the job. He flipped open his laptop, which had been sitting next to him, closed, on the couch, and clicked on Twitter. At first he didn't see much, just the usual stream of stuff that didn't make much sense to him.

"What are you talking about, T?"

And then he saw it. There was a Twitter trend—Jericho and Kerry—and it was like a damn magnet. There wasn't a chance in hell that he wasn't going to click on it.

"Kerry, you're looking, aren't you?"

"Of course I—oh." And that's when he saw it. Again.

There was tweet after tweet:

"Did Jericho dump Kerry? Who's that dude?"

"Awwww I loved them."

"That's definitely not Kerry. Maybe the other guy is just a friend."

Kerry's stomach dropped, but he didn't get it. He didn't get why they'd think that Jericho had broken up with him. Until he got to the pictures. There, in way too much detail, were pictures of Jericho at the "boring and crowded" afternoon pool party. He was on some velvety booth seat, sitting right next to this guy—blond, pretty, lanky—pretty much the opposite of Kerry. They weren't kissing or anything, and he supposed the pictures could look completely innocent but Kerry knew that face. He knew how Jericho looked at someone when he was into them. Jericho looked at the blond man like he wanted to kiss him. Kerry bit his lip to hold back tears.

"I have to go, T."

"Shit. Kerry. I'm coming over there."

"No. I… I'm sure there's a reason. I have to go, okay. I'll talk to you later."

Kerry waited for a text from Jericho. He had to know by then that the pictures were splashed all over the Internet. Pictures again. Wasn't that what started the whole mess in the first place?

Kerry took his tea and his laptop and wandered back upstairs to Jericho's room—the room he'd been sleeping in for weeks. It smelled like Jericho, and like him a little bit. It was warm with the last of the summer sun leaking through the windows. Kerry curled up in bed with his laptop and scrolled the Twitter tag obsessively. There were more angles—Jericho grinning a big flirtatious grin, kissing his cheek in greeting, head thrown back in laughter. Again, nothing that was concrete, but Kerry knew a brush off when he saw one and Jericho was making it very clear that he was interested in moving on. It hurt like hell, and he couldn't stop staring.

Part of him wasn't surprised. Jericho had been weird the past few days. Hot and then cold, sweet and then dismissive. He'd been pulling away, and Kerry had been trying hard not to hold tighter and tighter. The Jericho he'd had right after Charleston wasn't there anymore. He wanted him back more than anything. Looked like that wasn't going to happen.

But still, he couldn't stop looking.

It twisted in his belly until he felt like he was going to cry, but he couldn't stop scrolling through the comments. By that point, he had hundreds of mentions on his own timeline, fans asking if he and Jericho had broken up, some of his newly earned thousands of Twitter followers demanding an explanation. Kerry didn't know what to do. The PR person in him wondered if he should ignore it, wondered if he should explain something that he couldn't explain. The regular guy in him, the one who'd fallen so deeply in love, wanted to curl up in a little ball under the covers and die. He ended up doing the second thing, once he could force himself to close the computer and set it down on the floor away from him. He rolled under Jericho's light, expensive comforter and closed his eyes. He mashed his face into the pillow and tried not to cry. Didn't work so well.

Still, he must've fallen asleep, because it was dark when he woke to the sound of the door opening.

"JERICHO?" he called. Kerry didn't get an answer until Jericho was right in the doorway. He looked rough and a little cold. Kind of reminded Kerry of the Jericho from the beginning of summer. "What's wrong?"

Jericho shrugged. "Nothing."

Oh, shit. Kerry knew he'd been right when he saw the pictures – a brush off just like he'd thought. It wasn't good. He scooted up until he was sitting and swung his legs over the side of the bed.

"What's going on with you?" he asked.

"Like I said. Nothing. Just blowing off a little steam before I leave. I start filming on Monday."

Blowing off steam. Right. He knew the look on Jericho's face before he even asked. Something had happened.

"So...."

"So what?"

Kerry could barely bring himself to say it. "You and me."

"I kind of thought that our little game was over. I mean, I *am* leaving, and we did what we set out to do. Is there something else?"

Is there something else....

"Jericho, we haven't been papped for weeks, not since we got home from Charleston. This whole time that was just...."

"I guess a reward for a job well done." Jericho raised his eyebrow like he almost dared Kerry to contradict him. Kerry loved Jericho. He'd come to that realization days ago. He loved him with everything he had, but he also had pride. He wasn't going to act like a fool over this guy who clearly didn't want anything but a ticket out the door.

"A reward. Awesome." Kerry stood and gathered the clothes he'd draped over Jericho's chair the night before.

"Hey, listen. I was thinking of leaving a little early, like the morning probably, but there's no reason you should suffer the last of the warm weather without a pool. Feel free to stay here as long as you like. I'll let Debbie know to keep the fridge stocked."

"That's not necessary," Kerry choked out. If he had his way, he'd be gone in an hour. Less. It was like whiplash. A few hours ago, he'd been puttering around

Jericho's house, feeling settled and domestic, and all of a sudden, he was ready to shove his crap in a bag and get the hell out of there.

He nodded at Jericho, the cold, laid-back Jericho who he hadn't seen since June, and he made his way down the spiral stairs, nearly tripped and face planted, but finally got to his old guest room. He'd only been in and out of there to change clothes. He hoped it wouldn't take too long to pack.

JERICHO felt horrible. Like there was a hole inside him that was slowly filling with acid and only running after Kerry and getting his happiness back would make it stop. But then he remembered the words. *Pussy. Whipped. Bitch boy...* and he remembered the pain of his skull cracking against the metal grate of his locker in school, and he stopped himself. He stood up in his room for a good half an hour until he heard the front door close and Kerry's car start up in the driveway. Then he slid down the wall of his bedroom and collapsed onto the floor. He had to make Kerry leave but it hurt like hell.

Chapter Twelve

KERRY didn't know how he was going to let it go—Jericho, their time together, this life. All of it. Kerry hadn't ever really had his heart broken before. He'd had breakups in the past of course, but it wasn't like this. When they ended, it was with a vague sadness and probably more relief. Every second, every piece of clothing he put away, all of it. It hurt. Like deep claws in his skin, ripping and pulling kind of hurt. Kerry hated it.

He'd always wanted to know what it felt like to really fall in love—to feel the belly flip and the loss of control. He wished he could take it back. Falling in love was the worst idea ever, and Kerry hated it. More than anything he wished to rewind to the beginning of summer, find another guy to play Jericho's fiancé, and never feel what he felt right that second. He'd trade the loss of that giddy rush back in a heartbeat if it meant he could avoid this angry violent humiliation. He'd acted like such a lovesick fool. He hadn't thought he was in it alone. Obviously, he'd been wrong, and he wanted to take it all back. Nothing was worth the feeling of utter heartbreak that he should've seen coming from a mile away.

But he'd have to move on.

He shoved the last of his things into a bag and waited. The paps weren't around much anymore. It was still better to wait for the cover of dark. He'd get into his crappy car, the one that had been in a garage for the better part of two months, and he'd slip into the night like he'd never been there at all.

Kerry was having a hard time sitting still. He pulled all the sheets off the bed and left them for the housekeeper, who'd told him not to worry about it. Then he smoothed the comforter back into place and looked out the window. It was dark enough. Kerry couldn't stand being there any longer.

He slung his bags over his shoulder and jingled his keys, lighter now that the set to his temporary car were sitting on the kitchen counter; then he keyed in Jericho's alarm code, locked up the house, and left.

THE drive back to reality seemed to take hours. It felt like there was this rubber band around him, around his car, making it impossible to distance himself from Jericho's house without wanting to pull back. Eventually he knew the band would break, and he'd be free. He just didn't know how long that would take. Finally, though, Kerry found a spot in his building's parking lot, hiked his bags over his shoulder, and made his way up to the apartment.

It looked different, after everything he'd been through. Small, which was expected, but also a lot more homey, which wasn't. He'd gotten used to Jericho's. He'd been happy there in the final weeks. Deliriously happy. But in a weird way, he was still glad to be home. The guys were out—Robbie at his first night-league lacrosse game of the season, and Cole at celebratory drinks for finishing the first week of his new job. Kerry had been invited, but he'd said he'd help celebrate later, and that he was beat. His brother and Robbie were growing up, moving on, finishing school and becoming adults. Kerry felt stuck. He should be further along in his life. Instead he felt, somehow, like he was starting over. Or maybe he just wanted to start over. He sank down into the magic sofa spot. It wasn't as comfortable as he remembered.

Kerry sat there in silence for a few minutes before he decided he might as well go put his clothes away. It was lucky he'd decided to wash them earlier, since he hadn't had much else to do. Kerry hung shirts and jeans, folded sweats and socks, and put them into drawers. It was bittersweet, he decided. He was happy to be home. He was. He just didn't know how long home was going to last as it was. Robbie would move on. Cole would move on. He… needed to do the same. Just, how?

He'd finished putting his clothes away and was back on the couch by the time Robbie showed up. Robbie wasn't the most sensitive, but it must've been obvious how unhappy Kerry was. He just sat down on the couch next to him, offered chips, and helped him watch whatever crap show he'd turned on when he sat down. Cole came about a half an hour later. He was buzzed off a few beers and the high of starting a new life. Still, he took one look at Kerry and scowled.

"You want me to go kick his ass, because I honestly think I'd have fun doing it."

"No." Kerry smiled. "He didn't do anything wrong. I'm the one who broke my own damn heart."

"Don't say that."

"What? This was always business for him, from start to finish. He said it a million times. We had a contract. No part of that contract said Jericho Knox is required to fall in love with his inexperienced, fake publicity fiancé." Kerry told himself that he believed every word he'd just said. He didn't. There had been something real. He wasn't hallucinating everything.

"But he did. He's in love with you, Bro."

"Don't...."

"I agree with Cole," Robbie said. "Nobody looks at someone like that if they aren't in love."

"He's an actor. Let's not forget that."

"Right. And he was acting when we were over at the pool?"

Or the night they kissed for the first time, or when Jericho had taken him to bed on the island. The night that Kerry thought everything had changed.

"I honestly don't know, guys. But either way, it's over and I have to move on."

"I hate him," Cole said.

"I don't. Not yet." Kerry honestly wished he could.

KERRY got a promotion on Monday morning. Full-time part of the team, no more tweets, no more running errands for the others. He'd even get his own clients.

Somehow it didn't feel the way he'd thought it would feel. It felt pretty horrible actually.

It had taken a while to realize how much he hated his job—maybe being on the other side of the table, actually participating in all the horrible things they set up for the clients. Some didn't seem to mind it, all the faking and the paps stalking their every move, but it didn't make Kerry feel better as a person. He wanted out. He just didn't know where the hell he'd go just yet. So he stayed. And took the promotion, the much better paycheck, and the task of finding someone to replace his old position.

Tara had kept her word to get Oscar out. He was gone by the end of the week. The office was better without his bitching, but it didn't make Kerry want to stay.

It wasn't like he was going to be happy anyway, so he did.

September felt like three years. He got his first client and ran some simple publicity outings for her, found a new replacement grunt to do his old job, even went to a few events with Tara. He tried to feel something other than vague disgust. It hadn't happened yet.

October… was basically the same as September. Cole and Robbie had jobs, and they were up to their neck in new adulthood, so Kerry didn't see them much. He spent more time at the gym, tried to wear himself out so he could sleep at night without waking up when he thought he felt Jericho's breath bathing his neck. After the dreams, when he'd forget that he was alone, he'd lie there awake and wish for one more hug, another kiss, a final shared shower full of slippery skin and giggling kisses. Sometimes it seemed like it couldn't really be over. That Kerry had to have imagined how Jericho just walked away with a shrug like none of it had ever happened. But he hadn't. And when the sun came up, he'd get up, get dressed, and go to work like every other day—quite often Saturdays and Sundays too—and try to push the summer out of his mind.

One afternoon in the middle of November, Tara came into his office, the one he'd still never gotten used to having, and shut the door behind her. She locked it too and faced Kerry with a determined scowl. Tara, sunny Tara, never frowned, it seemed. Kerry didn't know what to do.

"We need to talk," Tara said.

"Are you breaking up with me?" Kerry asked. He pouted and tried to make her laugh. He wasn't in the mood for an intervention, and he knew he was getting one if he didn't play his cards right.

"Don't try to joke with me."

"Fine. *No* joking. What's wrong?"

"You tell me."

Kerry sighed. He felt like everyone would know, like his insides were plastered all over his skin for the whole world to see. He could've told Tara everything, how his heart literally ached, like he was aware of it thumping along bruised and battered in his chest, how he didn't have the energy to do anything, how eating felt like a chore and half the time he skipped it, how he couldn't close his eyes without seeing Jericho's face. He didn't tell her all of that. Instead he just shrugged.

"I guess I'm a little worn out. A new job comes with a lot of different responsibilities that I didn't have before."

"Bullshit."

"Tara Tiara, did you just swear?"

"I'm worried about you, Kerry. So is Abby. You're not yourself anymore, and we both think we know why."

"Then what was the point of asking me?" Kerry wasn't in the mood for a lecture. He was *trying*. He'd gotten to the point where he wasn't sad anymore, where he didn't want to wake up and find out that it was a bad dream, and he was back with Jericho. He was past that and more into the hatred-and-never-again phase. But he was still trying to get over it. It wasn't easy.

"I just wanted to give you the opportunity to say it yourself before the intervention."

"What intervention?"

"Abby and I are taking you out to find a boy. You need to wash Jericho Knox off your skin, and there's only one proven way to do that."

"I'm not that guy, T. I've never been that guy."

"I'm guessing you've also never been the guy who fell so hard he could barely see straight either. Have you?"

"No."

"Then this calls for drastic measures. You need a Jericho cleanse."

Kerry knew he wasn't going to get rid of her until he at least agreed to the going out part. There wasn't a chance in hell he was going to sleep with some random guy. People still recognized him. People still thought he was with Jericho. At least that's what Kerry told himself.

"Can I at least go home and change out of my office clothes?"

"Yeah, I'll come with you."

"Tara, I can go change and shower on my own."

"Right. And then when you're conveniently there, and I'm here, you'll call and say you're tired, and I wasn't born bloody yesterday Kerry Pickering."

"Bloody?"

She sighed. "I've been spending a little too much time with that new tennis player we're repping lately. His damn dialect is rubbing off on me."

Kerry snorted. "Well, cheerio old chap. I'm pretty much wrapped up. You really want to follow me all the way home?"

"Yep. And I'll text Abby when we're heading back out."

"My apartment isn't amazing. And Cole might be there if he's off of work." Not that he thought his brother was a creepy stalker, but he'd do just about anything to get Tara to leave him to his misery.

"Maybe he can come too. I'm sure he'd like to see you get over that ass."

"He's not an ass." Kerry could hate him, but he didn't want other people talking about him like that.

"Really?"

"No. He just…."

"Broke your heart? Led you on?"

"Okay. Maybe he's a huge ass. Or maybe I just expected too much."

"Bullshit," she said again.

"Come on. Let's go before traffic gets too bad."

"I didn't know there was a time period before that happened," Tara said.

"Good point."

JERICHO should have been happy. He knew he should be happy. He was in the middle of doing everything he'd always wanted—awesome role, great cast, and he really liked Vancouver and had no problem making it his home for a large part of the year. He'd even been seeing someone about his newly returned high school issues after he'd broken down to his mom, and she'd practically told him she'd come up there and drag him to a therapist herself if he didn't start going. She'd sounded angry, but Jericho knew she was scared. So he went. And it had helped a lot. But... he wasn't happy. He was more than not happy; he was miserable. And he knew why.

It had been three months. Three months since he pulled out of Los Angeles, and three months since he'd seen Kerry. It felt like he was starving. He sat in his trailer during break and read through the lines. He had a pivotal scene with Wiley next, action with intense dialogue and even some fight choreography, and he had to nail it. He'd been doing really well, according to everyone. Seemed like this new brand of being miserable didn't coincide with him ruining his career like the last one did.

There was a knock on his trailer door. Jericho put down his script. "Come in!" he called.

"Hey, man. Just seeing what was up." Wiley was standing outside his trailer, still in full costume.

"I'm just trying to block out the next scene in my head. Do they need me?"

"No, you're fine. Or rather... you're not. I'm worried about you, man. What's going on?"

"Are my scenes falling flat? I was kind of worried about that last one with—"

"No, your scenes are great. You're doing really well, okay? It's not that." Wiley smiled and clapped him gently on the shoulder.

"What is it?"

"You tell me. You were glowing this summer when I saw you at that party. Glowing. And now you seem like the glow got put out. And Kerry hasn't been up here once. Don't tell me you two are over."

"Wiley, we were never a thing in the first place." Jericho shrugged. "I know they're going to slowly break us up in the papers and wherever else they do all that stuff, but they wanted to let me get settled on the show first. It was all a stunt." It hurt like hell to say. Which was probably why he hadn't told his old friend the whole story yet.

Wiley burst out laughing. Turned out he was about as easy to fool as Jericho's mother. "Bullshit. I know what a publicity relationship looks like. You two were the real deal."

"I love him," Jericho said quietly. It was the first time he'd said it out loud. The first time he'd let himself think about why he was miserable in such clear words. "I broke up with him for real, and it was the worst mistake I've ever made in my life."

Jericho waited for the noises in his head, for the guys shouting at him, calling him names, but the only thing he could see was Kerry's heartbroken face when Jericho pretended he was bored with what they had. It had been so opposite from true. Jericho's fingers still ached for Kerry's skin.

"Then why did you tell me you'd drive down to Seattle for that Seahawks game with me this weekend? What the hell are you doing here?"

"Working?"

Wiley snorted hard. "Get on a plane when you're done with your last scene. Go to LA. Get your boy."

"Wiley…."

Wiley held up his hand. "I really fucking liked the version of you I met this summer. I'd like for him to be my coworker. I like you too, but I think we both need him back."

Jericho groaned. "I fucked things up. He's not going to take me back."

"I have faith," Wiley said. "You'll work it out."

Chapter Thirteen

JERICHO was nervous on the airplane, he was nervous in the car, and when he showered at his place—which felt like he'd lived there in another lifetime—and changed into jeans, a shirt, and a jacket, he felt his belly screw up into a little tight ball of fear. By the time he got into the elevators at Jones & Keller, he felt like turning around and running as fast as he could. But he had to do it. He needed to see Kerry. It might have been the most impulsive thing he'd ever done, but it was important too.

He got off the elevator at the fourth floor, and that's when he stalled. He realized he never really knew where in the office Kerry worked. It wasn't *that* big, but he didn't feel like knocking on doors, one after the other. Luckily he saw Tara, walking down the hallway in one of her flowing shirts and a tight pair of jeans with boots.

"Jericho." She didn't look pleased to see him. "What are you doing here?"

"I need to talk to Kerry. Which of these is his office?"

"He's not here. He went to get lunch." Tara didn't look like she was going to give him a break.

"I'll wait for him, Tara. I just… I really need to talk to him."

She scowled. "I'm not sure I want that. You broke his heart, Jericho. You know you did."

"Yeah, and in the process I broke my own heart too." He wasn't going to stand in the hallway and spill his damn guts out to Tara, whom he barely knew. "Can you please just tell me which one his office is?"

She gave him a long sigh. "It's the one in the corner. His name is on the door, and he never remembers to lock it."

Jericho walked down to the corner office that did say Kerry Pickering right on the door plaque. He opened it and found that Tara was right. It was unlocked.

The office didn't look very lived in. There was a box in the corner and no pictures on the wall. Nothing about it said Kerry. There was a soft leather chair in the corner, though, so Jericho took a seat on it and waited.

He waited for nearly an hour before the door cracked open, and *Jesus*, he hadn't expected that kind of impact.

Kerry.

He was still gorgeous and compact, his hair was still dark and shiny, but he was *thin*. Far thinner than he'd been in September, and he looked tired and pale in a way he'd never been pale before.

"Ke—"

Kerry jumped and choked off a scream. Then he noticed who it was, and he narrowed his eyes.

"What the hell are you doing here?" he asked. His voice was cold. The ice burned.

"I need to talk to you."

"I can't imagine what about." He was so *cold*. Even before, when he'd been annoyed and angry with Jericho, when he'd barely been able to keep his patience, he'd never been this icy. Jericho knew it was his fault.

"Kerry, you know what about. I'm sorry. I needed to tell you I'm sorry."

"Sorry for what? Letting me fall in love with you, encouraging it when you never meant for a damn thing to come of us?" Kerry laughed. It was humorless and just as cold as his voice. "Yeah, I was in love with you. Didn't seem to be too bothered by it when you were fucking me. Maybe you can find another fake boyfriend to fuck. One who's better for your image than some kid from a PR firm. You know… I can even help you with that. After the stellar job I did with your image, I've been promoted to deal directly with talent."

It felt like Jericho had been stabbed.

"You want…."

"I want you to go. Please."

Jericho didn't know what to say. So he didn't say anything. He simply turned and walked back down the hall, got on the elevator, and left.

It wasn't until he was in his car, driving back to his house, that Jericho let it hit him. He'd ruined everything. It was over.

"WILEY, it's over. I'm on my way back."

"What are you talking about, man?"

Jericho sighed. "I tried. I tried to talk to him, and he told me he didn't want to see me. I just… I didn't know what to do, so I left his office. It's over."

Wiley had the balls to laugh. "You mean you tried to get him back one time only, and you're giving up?"

"Yes?"

Jericho didn't know what the hell was so funny.

"Man, you're not coming back here. Try again. What did he look like?"

"Cold. Kind of angry. He told me he could set me up with another PR boyfriend."

"Ouch. But if he was swiping at you like that, he still feels things. That anger was hurt. And hurt means you might get another chance."

"I don't want to be creepy."

"You won't. Can you get him to your place? That way if he comes, he's at least okay with that."

"I do have a necklace he left here back in the fall." He'd taken it to Vancouver with him. Jericho hated to admit he kind of wore it everywhere.

"Good. Ask if he'll stop by to pick it up. Give it another chance. At least one more. You deserve that."

"Okay. Thanks, man."

"I'll see you in a couple of days. Hopefully you'll have Kerry with you."

"I'm not so sure about that."

Wiley chuckled. "I have faith."

KERRY'S hands were sweating. It was like that feeling when he'd been away at school for a long time, and he'd gone back for the holidays. Everything felt the same, he knew where his high school was, and the grocery store, and the mall, and his friends' houses, and people were where they belonged for the most part, and everything looked like it had been ticking along just fine.

But it wasn't just fine.

It was different. Everything was.

That's what the drive to Jericho's felt like. Different.

He hadn't been there since early September, three long months. He'd tried to cut Jericho out of his life in every way. And it had worked. To a point. He still got stopped on the street, people asked him how Jericho was doing with his new show and when he was going to go visit. They hadn't followed through with the breakup procedure yet, so he just lied. Said Jericho was happy, he'd been to see him a few times, the set was great, blah, blah, blah.

Which was right.

Blah.

That's how Kerry's life had felt for months. He didn't know what to do about it. He kept waiting for that day when he was going to pop out of bed and feel normal for once, like he did before Jericho fucking Knox burst into his life and tore it into little strips so it could fit around him. Kerry didn't think the strips would ever sew back so they fit just him anymore. Not after so much wear and tear.

He thought about moving home to Oxnard.

Kerry literally hated going to work every day. He didn't want his job anymore, not even a little bit. He thought that going home would be like giving up, though, and he wasn't ready to be the biggest loser in Los Angeles.

He turned down the long, winding road that ended at Jericho's drive. His stomach tied itself up in knots.

Do I really need that necklace back?

His first instinct when he got the text was to ignore it. Even seeing the house would hurt too much. But the necklace was important. It had been a gift from Cole when he'd graduated from college. Yes. He needed it. He wished he didn't. Jericho had promised he'd get the maid to just leave it on the front portico. That shouldn't be too painful. Pick up the necklace and move on with the rest of his life. No problem, right?

Kerry was a little surprised that he still knew the gate code. The months he'd been with Jericho almost felt like some kind of… battle. He was sure as hell scarred from it. Kerry had a habit of forgetting things when he was under duress. But he knew the gate code as well as he knew his own phone number. And he pulled up the drive and parked, and it felt so familiar. Not like the hometown feeling anymore, but actually familiar like he belonged there. It felt right. Too bad it wasn't, and Jericho wasn't, and everything he'd been hoping back in the summer was absolutely never going to happen.

He forced himself to get out of the car. Get it over with. Kerry pulled the loose key out of his pocket and headed up to the front portico. He'd been told his necklace would be in a bag on the bench. There was no bag on the bench.

Wonder if the housekeeper thought Jericho meant the kitchen counter. Bench meant counter sometimes, right?

Kerry didn't want to go in, but if he left, he'd chicken out, and his necklace would never find its way home. His hands shook as he knocked on the door. It swung open.

"Hello?" he called. Nothing.

"Are you looking for this?"

Kerry nearly screamed. Jericho stood right there, right there like some kind of goddamn mirage with Kerry's necklace dangling from his finger.

"You were supposed to be flying up north by now. Why are you here?"

Jericho shrugged. "I just am. And you are too."

"Y-yeah. I am." Kerry didn't know what the hell he was supposed to say. What was Jericho doing there? Why wasn't he in Vancouver? "You didn't get fired, did you?"

Jericho laughed. "Not much faith in my skills, Little K."

He'd only called him that a couple of times, usually in bed, sated, happy. "Please don't call me that."

Jericho's face twisted.

"Can I have my necklace, please? Cole gave it to me for graduation. It's kind of important."

Jericho handed Kerry the necklace. The chain felt warm and solid in his hand. The only warm, solid thing Kerry had to hold on to. He was spinning. He turned to leave, figured there wasn't anything else to say.

"Can you wait?" Jericho asked.

"W-what?" What the hell did he want? What could he possibly want?

"I said, can you wait?"

"Why?"

"I think we need to talk."

Kerry's hand started trembling. "Don't you think we did enough of that back in September?" he asked.

"No. I think I said all the wrong things to you back in September. That's not what should have happened."

Kerry was getting a little annoyed. "I don't know what you want from me here, Jericho."

"Jay," Jericho said quietly. "I told you to call me Jay."

"That was a different life," Kerry said. "A mirage."

Jericho moved closer, slowly but steadily. "I don't want those months to be a mirage. It was the happiest I've ever been. I miss it. I miss *you*."

"What?" Kerry felt like a broken record. "You said...."

"I know what I said. I lied."

"You can't just do that to people, Jericho." Kerry stopped and thought for a moment. "Wait. What did you lie about?"

Jericho shrugged. "All of it?"

"Why?" He didn't even know if he wanted to hear it, but part of him needed to.

"Because I'm an asshole." Jericho laughed bitterly. "Because I let some guy say one thing to me and turn me into the insecure teenager I've been running away from all these years."

"I don't get it."

Jericho sighed. "I told you I was nerdy, right?" Kerry nodded. "I didn't tell you I was bullied. For being gay."

"So you want to stay closeted?" Kerry was confused.

"Of course not. You know that. I guess," Jericho looked like he didn't know how to continue. "I guess I never blamed the beatings on being gay. That's just who I was. I blamed it on being weak. I let those guys get to me and I swore I'd never let anyone get under my skin again. But you *did*. In such an amazing way."

"So what happened."

"I barely want to admit it."

"You're gonna have to. I need to hear this. I need to hear why you hurt me so badly."

"Because this dickhead at a party called me a pussy for falling for you. He sounded so much like those guys at home and I was so in love with you, *am* so in love with you. It scared me. I ran when that should've been the last thing I did. It was the worst mistake I ever made. I want to be with you. I've always wanted to be with you."

"This isn't fair. *I've* just spent the last three months trying to get over you."

Jericho's face crumpled. "And did you? Get over me?"

Kerry wanted to say yes so badly, turn around and get out of there. But somehow he couldn't lie. It was like his body wouldn't let him make that mistake. Was it a mistake? Who even knew that?

"No. I didn't." He looked at the ground. He couldn't stand to look up at Jericho and hope for something that he knew wasn't going to happen. Jericho, of course, wouldn't let him avoid it.

"Babe," Jericho said. "I didn't get over you either. What we had was…."

"What? Easy sex before you left for your real life on the TV set?" Kerry spat. "You should be able to get that just as easily from the boys in Vancouver."

"No. No. I'd never do that." Jericho pulled Kerry into a tight hug. Kerry stood there frozen for a minute. He didn't know what to do. "Please hug me back," Jericho whispered. "I couldn't take it if you won't even touch me."

Kerry glanced up sharply at his heartbroken voice. "Please."

He slowly wound his arms around Jericho's waist and hugged him. It took a while to melt back in, to feel what he'd felt when they were together before, but it was all there—the warmth of his skin where Kerry nosed into his neck, the way he smelled, how his arms were strong but gentle. Jericho's hugs were part of his body memory. Kerry didn't know what to think of that.

"What are we doing?" he whispered. Kerry wasn't mentally prepared.

"I'm trying to tell you that I'm still in love with you," Jericho said. "I was in love with you back in the summer, and I probably will be in forty years too."

"Not fifty?" Kerry asked. He couldn't help the smile that bubbled up from somewhere inside him where he hadn't lost hope.

"I don't know. We'll have to take stock then." Jericho smiled. "I'm so sorry, babe. Like, you have no idea how sorry. I've been miserable for months, beating myself up for the way I treated you. My mom was right. You're the best thing that ever happened to me, and I don't think I can do this without you anymore."

"You really love me?" Kerry asked. It was so surreal.

"Yes. And if you're not ready to say that back to me yet, I get it. But all I want is the chance to try. If you'll let me."

Kerry did love Jericho, of course. He'd loved him since… he didn't know when it had happened. "I do."

"You do what? Want to let me?"

"No. I do love you. I've spent three months wishing I didn't, but apparently wishing doesn't make it go away."

That was all it took. Jericho pulled him into the tightest squeeze Kerry had ever received. He was trembling, and Kerry wasn't sure if he those were tears dropping on the top of his head. Kerry sort of felt like crying himself, so he got it.

"I love you too." Jericho's voice sounded stuffy and thick. "Jesus. What's wrong with me?" He laughed.

"It's okay. I get it." Kerry wiped his eyes off too. "I just… wasn't expecting this today."

"I should've done it months ago. I don't want to be away from you ever again. Will you have me?"

"Yeah." Kerry didn't even want to say no.

THEY kissed after that, then smiled, laughed, kissed a little more, maybe shed a few tears. Then they unwrapped each other and sank into Jericho's bed where things had always seemed right and easy. Where skin touched skin, and Kerry's real life never seemed to intrude.

"I missed being engaged to you," Jericho said with a soft smile when they were sweaty and sated and happy.

Kerry chuckled. "I missed being engaged to you too."

"I want to do it for real someday soon."

"Yeah?" Kerry tried to smile to cover up the way his heart was pounding.

"Definitely."

"Me too." He rubbed his face against Jericho's chest.

"Hey, Kerry?"

"Yeah."

"What would be the chances that George would let you telecommute from Vancouver for a little while?"

"Not very much."

"Oh." Jericho looked disappointed. "I have to go back on Monday. I don't want to leave you."

"Well, it doesn't matter anyway, because I quit today."

"What?"

"I hated that job. I didn't realize how much I didn't want to do it until I was with you. I told you I got a promotion after you left? It felt like the worst news ever. That's when I knew I was done."

"So you're…."

"Jobless for the moment. And apparently mooching off my brother, who refuses to let me move home with Mom and Dad."

Kerry didn't know why he was hesitant to move back to Oxnard. It would be practical; he'd be able to find a retail job, save some money. Start over. It just felt like giving up somehow. Especially after everything he'd been through.

Jericho smiled slowly. "How 'bout you try Canada for a little while?"

"With you?"

"Yeah. With me."

"What would I do up there?"

"Let me spoil you. Find a job if you want to. Whatever you want, just… come with me."

Kerry thought about it for ten seconds, maybe twenty. But he already knew the answer.

"Okay. I'll come to Vancouver."

"Really?" Jericho looked so sweet and open, like a kid who'd just gotten everything he wanted.

"Yeah. I could use an adventure."

"And me? Do you really want to be with me?"

"That too."

Coming in September 2016

DREAMSPUN DESIRES

#17

The Senator's Secret by K.C. Wells

The campaign is heating up.

When his Republican opponent outs him with a photo in a Facebook post, Senator Samuel Dalton doesn't have many options open to him. It doesn't matter that the photo is totally innocent. He has no choice but to come clean—until his staff suggest putting a spin on it that leaves Sam reeling.

Sure, he'll end up with a lot of sympathy, not to mention the possibility of more voters from the LGBT community, but it still seems a pretty drastic solution.

Now all they have to do is persuade Gary, the other man in the photo, to play along. It sounds so easy—convince the constituents of North Carolina that he and Sam are engaged.

No big deal, except for the fact that they've only just met….

#18

Commitment Ranch by BA Tortuga

A fist fight, a snowstorm, a stolen kiss in the barn... and a second chance at love.

Ford Nixel has two law offices, two fancy condominiums, and all the right connections. In short, he has everything he wants.

The last thing he needs is his Uncle Ty's stake in the Leaning N, a dude ranch that's been in the family for generations. Ford hasn't even been to the ranch in a decade, not since he left behind his boyfriend, Stoney, to head back to college alone.

Ford arrives at the Leaning N to find Stoney, now a single father, right where he left him—a fist fight, a snow storm, and a stolen kiss in the barn later, Ford knows none of the heat between them has dissipated.

www.dreamspinnerpress.com

Now Available

#13
Ace in the Hole by Ava Drake
A Wild Cards Novel

Love on the Edge.

Christian Chatsworth-Brandeis has a problem. A huge one. The US senator he works for has run away with his latest mistress on the eve of a make-or-break fund-raising event, and it's up to him to cover his boss's irresponsible tracks.

Stone Jackson, the senator's new bodyguard, looks enough like the senator that, with some extensive grooming, he might pass for Senator Lacey. Christian and Stone hatch a plan to fool everyone by substituting Stone for the senator, but Miami madness and the incendiary heat between them are throwing obstacles in their way. It's a race to find the senator and pull off the con of the century before the attraction between them spins completely out of control.

#14
The Greek Tycoon's Green Card Groom by Kate McMurray

Marriage gets less convenient when love is involved.

It started simple: Ondrej Kovac marries Archie Katsaros so Ondrej can stay in the US, away from his judgmental family in eastern Europe. Archie marries Ondrej in exchange for the money to bail out his failing company. It's a fraud neither man is convinced he can pull off.

But as Archie introduces Ondrej to New York society and Ondrej proves his skill in the office, they start to discover a connection between them. Can they overcome the rocky foundation their relationship was built on, meddling immigration agents, gossip columnists determined to out their deception, and an aggressive executive set on selling Archie's company out from under him? Only if they can prove to each other their love is worth fighting for.

www.dreamspinnerpress.com

Love Always Finds a Way

DREAMSPUN DESIRES

Subscription Service

Love eBooks?

Our monthly subscription service gives you two eBooks per month for one low price. Each month's titles will be automatically delivered to your Dreamspinner Bookshelf on their release dates.

Prefer print?

Receive two paperbacks per month! Both books ship on the 1st of the month, giving you *exclusive* early access! As a bonus, you'll receive both eBooks on their release dates!

Visit
www.dreamspinnerpress.com
for more info or to sign up now!

CPSIA information can be obtained
at www.ICGtesting.com
Printed in the USA
BVHW071557100919
558045BV00003B/293/P